STRANDS OF STARFIRE

REIGN

MAY SAGE

Strands of Starfire: Reign

May Sage © 2018

eBook ISBN: 978-1-912415-37-3
Paperback ISBN: 978-1-912415-28-1

ONE
THE NEW LORD

It wasn't often that Lord Kai smiled, but that day should have been one of those rare occasions. He'd won. He'd accomplished his goal. After over ten years, he stood on the High Throne in the cold castle dominating the planet-wide city of Vratis, fort to the Warlord of Ratna.

He'd defeated his enemy—almost all of his enemies. Those who oppressed and allowed others to live under the talon of slavery had answered for their crimes. Children with magic in their blood, condemned to death because of what they were, would be free now.

And yet, Kai's features were as expressionless as ever. Not even a hint of a smile.

Kai Lor, of the House of Hora, got up from the

strange floating throne. Catching his intention, the responsive, coveted seat moved slowly to the floor. Now that he was at his companions' level, his tall stature seemed even more imposing. Evris, be they male or female, stood taller than most creatures in the known universe, and Kai had yet to meet anyone who reached past his shoulders. This alone might have made him seem threatening, but there was something else about him—in the way he moved and in his intense gaze, perhaps. Those who met him for the first time generally knew to fear him. Those who were familiar with him, even more so.

The room only served to aggravate his fearsome persona. It was austere, like a temple, rather than the command center of a warlord. Kai didn't like it much. He'd have to get it redesigned; change all the purple lighting to red and paint the black walls white.

His four advisors and the seven guards, who'd spent the last hour arguing about the next step, grew silent when he descended the dais. He didn't bother to explain himself, leaving them to warily watch him head to the round balcony set at the back of the throne room.

The large beast that had rested on the platform over which the throne hovered lifted its head before trailing Kai's steps, following him out. It didn't fear him, unlike everyone else in the room.

The streets were eerily quiet below. This world

didn't yet know what sort of person their new master would be. They'd heard rumors. Terrible rumors. All of Vratis watched in an uneasy silence. By dawn, Kai would have more orders to give. He'd earn himself new enemies.

His fingers threaded through the rough bluish-silver fur of his snow wolf, his companion. The beast was the closest thing he had to real kin.

Kai frowned. That wasn't exactly true. There was one person who belonged at his side. Back when he'd seen her through the eyes of a seer, he'd known, without any doubt, that the female was meant to be with him—always. She was there, somewhere. He'd find her. He'd destroy worlds until she stood next to him.

The door of the throne room slid open behind him, and without leaving the balcony or turning to check, Kai knew it was Wench, his head mechanic. His aptitudes extended to feeling people around him. With experience, he'd learned to identify the vibe they emanated. Wench was steady and loyal. He felt like a deeply rooted tree.

"Where's the lord?"

The lord. That was him now.

"Out," someone replied, waving toward the curved doors leading to the balcony.

The man's confident steps had an upbeat ring as he rushed to the balcony. Kai wasn't surprised when he told him, "Good news!" Kai turned to him, brow lifted. "We found the child."

That caught and retained his attention.

Kai'd had many reasons for leading the civil war against their previous warlord. One of them was a child—a child without whom he may not be alive today.

There had been no sign of the child in the palace when he'd arrived, and the previous warlord's men weren't talking. Kai knew that now, over a dozen years after their first meeting, she wasn't a child at all. She'd be a young female in her twenties.

But still, he would have recognized her. And everyone in this palace would have known who she was; the old warlord's secret weapon. When he'd failed to find her, he'd guessed that his predecessor had had her killed, rather than surrendering her to him. A last act of defiance. But that theory didn't quite fit with Wench's upbeat demeanor.

"She's alive then."

Strange. Nothing outwardly betrayed a change in him, but he could feel it. His indifference vanished, replaced by a keen interest, and underneath it all, there was something else. Something he hadn't felt for a long time.

Hope?

The corner of Kai's lips lifted a smidgen.

"You'll want to watch the recordings we've dug out," said his mechanic. "It's a long story."

TWO
ENERGY

T *wenty-four years ago.*

"KAI," Balu whispered, waking him up instantly. It didn't take much to pull him from his light, restless sleep. Bad things happened to those who didn't stay on their guard in Haimo. "Kai, he's coming."

The boy stiffened at his friend's warning. Balu needn't specify who he meant when he said "he" that way. "He" was Master Hora.

Akia Tai Hora was the fat, indulgent noble who owned Haimo. Yes, the entire planet. His ancestors had come from a trade background, and prospered so much through the entire sector that a warlord of old had declared them dukes of Haimo, a then unclaimed, yet rich planet-wide territory.

Lord Hora didn't visit all his slaves' homes. Kai's was different in many respects, and a little nicer than most. Although she was owned by Akia, the female who lived there had a few slaves at her service. Mae, Kai's mother, and lady of this home, was no doubt the most exquisite female amongst the slaves. She had smooth, spotless, golden skin and long dark hair—a rare physical characteristic in their land—and a mouth that didn't need any rouge. She certainly looked nicer than Akia's noble wife. Thus, as their lord and master, he used her as he saw fit. Even at nine years old, Kai knew of these things.

No one had told him, but he'd guessed, with repulsion, that the fat noble was his biological father. Many clues had led him to that conclusion. For one, in looks, he was quite similar to Veli, the master's legitimate son. Kai was a little darker, with black eyes and hair like his mother, but their features were nonetheless similar. Secondly, Kai had long ago realized that he was treated quite well for a slave. Boys his age normally labored in the dangerous mines or in the fields—a hard, relentless work. Haimo was situated far from the sun of their system, making it the coldest planet in their world. But instead of being condemned to such work, Kai, at age six, when he'd been deemed old enough to work away from his mother, had been sent as an apprentice in the forges.

Akia also had an interest in him. He talked to him and sometimes even ruffled his hair. Kai thoroughly washed after such distressing occurrences. And then there was his name. Akai, he'd been called, by someone so lazy they'd simply flipped around his sperm donor's name to form his. He started demanding to be called Kai right after connecting the dots.

Kai jumped out of his bed, and promptly proceeded to hide his things—things he made from scraps he found everywhere. Pieces of metal, broken glass. Anything he found that could be of use, he kept and fashioned into something else. His mother called him her little artist.

From time to time, Akia came to his room, and he'd order him to keep the trash away. Kai had never received a beating for disobedience, but he'd seen others take one. Two winters past, he'd seen a grown-up die after a workmaster struck him with an energy whip. Five blows was all it had taken. Kai certainly didn't wish to gamble away his life that way. He couldn't pinpoint why, but Kai really did wish to live. Although perpetuating his harsh existence might have seemed pointless, he had hope. Hope for something more someday. He'd heard of slaves who'd earned their freedom. Why not him?

Balu helped. The boy put things in his trunks and polished his boots as Kai washed his knees and hands with soap. Balu was eleven, having two years on Kai. The boy had made it out of an accident in the mines a year ago, but it had left him weak and with just one leg. Kai had watched his mother kneel in front of master Akia upon Balu's behalf. "He'll do just fine in the house as there're no stairs," she told him. "He'll work."

Kai understood why she'd begged that way. If she hadn't spoken for him, Balu would have been shot. For his own good, the workmasters would say. Then, they'd mince him and give his flesh to the vepkhia or the nekos used in the arena games. Occasionally feeding them Evris flesh made them more vicious, hungry for more of it.

Akia wasn't the worst master. He'd sighed at Mae's request, but he let the boy heal and then sent him to their home. Kai was glad; he'd never had a friend before. The other children hated him because they knew. They saw it in his eyes; they might be dark like his mother's, but their shape didn't lie. He was the pampered master's bastard.

Kai hurried downstairs, keeping his gaze on the floor once he'd reached the master.

"Ah. Here he is. Getting bigger every time I see him."

Kai didn't reply, knowing the remark wasn't for him. "Yes, sir," said Mae Lor, always formal and deferential.

"Do you work well at the forges, boy?"

"Yes, sir," Kai echoed, talking now that he'd been addressed directly.

"Good, good. Come here. Take this."

He held his hand up and received a bronze coin for his effort. A fortune.

"Well, I'm sure you've got a lot to do."

This, he knew, was his clue to leave the room, leave the house. He was dismissed. The master had business with his mistress.

Kai ran. There was nowhere for a boy to go at six in the morning, but he ran. He'd reached the end of the village, arriving in front of the endless barren landscape where white dunes extended as far as his eyes could see, and then further still. There was no town on the planet, just the Hora residence surrounded by simple, flat roofed, identical buildings where he kept the men and women he'd purchased to work until they died. The contrast between the off-white homes with rustic materials and the golden palace with all its towers and domes couldn't be overstated.

Kai had never stepped in the palace. Later that day, he would.

HE'D LEFT SO FAST he hadn't taken his coat,

mittens, or the brown hat his mother had knitted him the previous week for his birthday. To keep warm, he moved constantly, blowing hot air on his hands. He was used to the cold, but in the dead of the Haimo winter, it was biting.

"Little Akai?"

The familiar voice calling him belonged to old Kumi, one of the few females with wrinkles on a well-worn face. Their way of life didn't lead to longevity.

The elder didn't ask what he was doing out by himself at this hour; instead, she waved his way. "Come on in, I'll give you something hot."

He practically tripped in his hurry to accept that invitation. She made the best root and spices drinks.

An hour later, wearing Kumi's scarf, he headed to work. He liked it at the forge.

Haimo was a mineral planet, so most of the slaves went down to the mines to dig out ray crystals. Those laboring at the surface cut and loaded humongous blocks of stone—granite, limestone, alabaster—onto cargo ships. The riches of Haimo were sold all over the galaxy, even to the Imperials.

The very best crystals, the rarest stones, and all of the fyriron were kept and sent to the forges. Fyriron was silvery and smooth, yet stronger than gold. It took a higher temperature to melt it, and Kai had heard that only a handful of forges in the galaxy were equipped to cast it. The weapons they formed were meant for warlords and kings.

Kai rushed to his station, not bothering to disturb the head of the forges with a greeting. Isha Lor, his uncle, didn't care much for civilities in general, and it was twice as true when he was sharpening a newly made blade. There was that look in his eyes, pride and sadness all mixed together. Isha loved his craft, but while he might create these masterpieces, it wasn't his name engraved in one corner; it was their master's. The half dozen of workmasters stationed in the forges served as a reminder of their position in this world.

Kai liked Isha, although the feeling wasn't mutual. Kai had always been good at telling how people felt. His mother's brother watched him with some suspicion, as though he expected him to do something unforgivable any second. It didn't bother the child. He knew trust was earned. Someday, Isha would know he was good, reliable. Isha already nodded at his work from time to time.

Along with half a dozen other apprentices, Kai labored in silence for hours under the watchful eye of the workmaster assigned to the forges. Then came their break. Someone rang a bell in the distance, indicating their food was ready, and they had fifteen minutes to go fetch it and eat it.

Everyone hurried to secure their work before heading out toward the eating hall.

One apprentice rushed the process that day. Instead of properly locking the blade he was sculpting onto the overhead shelf, Fein just hurriedly crammed it there.

Kai turned and screamed, "No!" before anyone saw the trajectory of the weapon as it fell. The slaves froze. The workmaster turned and watched Kai, who was standing, hand outstretched.

The blade had been halted in its course, millimeters away from Isha's face.

He'd never forget his uncle's face. There was terror in his eyes.

Kai didn't understand. He couldn't comprehend what had happened. Why hadn't the blade fallen to pierce Isha's skull, like he'd felt it would? Like he'd *seen* it would.

But he knew why. He'd stopped it. Without touching it, he'd stopped the object in midair. He could feel it, feel his hold on the metal as surely as if his hand had been around it. It wasn't his hand holding it, though; it was his mind.

That was his last thought as the workmaster hit him hard with the hilt of his blaster. Kai fell unconscious and woke up in chains.

He'd never been here before, but he knew exactly where he stood. The marble walls, the tall statues, the gold on the ceiling were all too luxurious for any other edifice in Haimo. He was in the palace.

In front of him stood Akia and Veli.

Veli was older than Kai, a teenager. He watched him with unconcealed rage. Akia was simply cold. His expression betrayed nothing.

Somehow Kai knew that it was all a facade. Beneath the indifference and the disdain, there was one clear feeling emanating from both father and son.

Fear.

They feared him.

They should.

"How long have you had magic?"

Magic. Was that what that was? Kai's heart stopped. He'd heard of magic. He'd heard those who wielded it were dangerous and evil.

He knew that they were killed.

"I don't—"

"Don't lie, child."

He closed his mouth.

He had magic. He'd witnessed and felt it; why deny it? Kai was no liar.

"I don't suppose it matters." Akia gestured to his guard. "Lead the boy to the woods, tie him up. I won't curse this land by spilling magical blood. Let the beasts and the cold take him."

Kai knew he was going to die when they left him outside the village, tightly bound to a tree. He didn't cry. It felt... familiar, like he'd lived through this again and again.

Like he knew this wasn't the end. He'd come back. He glared at the master defiantly. However many times they destroyed him, he'd come back.

AWAY FROM THIS, in a system where slavery was outlawed—the only system of the sort in the whole of the Ratna Belt—she was born that day.

They called her Nalini, daughter of Moa and Claus Nova, lords of the Val, King and Queen of Itri. As she was the eldest child in a strong line, rooted right back to their original planet, the happy parents cried for their little princess, foreseeing that she would do great things.

They had no idea.

She opened her eyes—one was blue and the other

amber, almost gold—and every object in the room started to fly.

Then, they really cried, because there was only one fate for those of their kind born with magic in their veins.

Death.

AND YET, neither of those children were destroyed that day.

THREE
THE WISE

The villagers watched with silent grief as Kai was tied up, bound by the wrists high about his head. His mother was one of the last to leave, tears in her eyes. Not a word crossed her lips. His uncle stayed until everyone else was gone.

No one attempted to free him. He didn't expect them to. They would have been filmed doing it by the hundreds of drones flying around Haimo at any given time, and then they would have shared his fate.

"I always saw it in you," said Isha. The words weren't accusatory. He sounded sad. "You know just what to do when no one explains it. Things that take years to learn, things my most senior apprentices can't do, you mastered in minutes. I've heard that those with magic were faster than us. Smarter." His uncle shook his head. "I'm sorry."

Kai's lips were turning blue, and he couldn't feel his feet right then. The apology left him entirely cold, like everything else. He didn't reply, and, at long last, Isha left him.

By the time darkness came, he could barely keep his eyes open. When he closed them, it would be the end. At that point, Kai wished it would arrive quickly. The bitter frost had taken his heart, his blood, his very being.

Hours passed. He closed his eyes and tried, tried as hard as he could to find peace. But his heart was as weary as it was wary. He felt like his life wasn't his to give up. Not just his at least.

If he died today, someone else would die too. He couldn't explain it, even to himself, but he couldn't shake that strange notion. Kai searched inside him, digging deep for an explanation of any sort. He didn't find one. Instead, breathing slowly, calmly, serenely, he found something else. Something strong he'd not even begun to tap into. The instant he connected to it, it came to him.

Warmth. Fire.

Kai mistook the unexpected comfort for death at first, but his eyes opened and the confused boy stared at a flame floating right in front of his face, practically burning his frozen nose.

He watched it, taking in the impossibility in disbelief.

And he saw other things, too. A few feet away, beasts had come, attracted to the darkness and the smell of his flesh. A pack of snow wolves. Beautiful, terrible beasts. Had they been standing up, they would have reached the size of a grown Evris man; on all four, they were almost as tall as Kai. They stayed away from the slaves' village when the lights were on, but it was dark now. They'd no doubt sensed an easy prey.

The fire Kai had conjured made them pause.

Kai tried to think clearly, ignore the fear, the cold, the pain. The fire was doing nothing more than keeping the immediate dangers at bay, simply prolonging his suffering. He closed his eyes and attempted to coax it into listening to his will.

The flame moved upward and started licking at his bonds. The wolves approached now that it was out of the way.

"Goddess Light, *please* hurry," he muttered urgently.

The flames became more intense, eating at the rope faster. They should have burned his fingers; somehow, they didn't.

His hands were free by the time the closest wolf was upon him. Falling forward, as his weak, frozen limbs wouldn't carry him, he watched the animal pounce.

His hand reached out, like it had back at the forge, an instinctive movement that had little to do with what was occurring right then in the physical world. Energy flowed from him to the beast, half caring, gentle, and just as authoritative. *I won't hurt you,* it said, as well as a clear, simple order. *Submit.*

The wolf whimpered and dropped its head. The rest of the pack stilled, watching Kai with their bright, beady eyes. Then they all howled in one voice, and their stance relaxed. They didn't seem ready to pounce now.

"I take it I'm not dinner anymore."

That was good. Great, in fact. It didn't change the fact that he was going to die unless he got himself off-planet.

Struggling, Kai got painfully to his feet. His first steps were slow. Feeling warmer, warmer than he'd ever been outside, he started to jog in the direction of the palace hangar.

Kai was a little confused to see the wolves follow suit, but there was no time to question it.

His speed increased; in no time, he was standing in front of the hangars where the Hora kept their ships.

There were guards, four of them at the door. More inside, he knew it. *Twelve.* He could... feel them. Their life force. Their presence.

These guards stood between him and his freedom. His very existence.

Both of Kai's hands lifted this time. Then he closed his fists, an automatic movement that yet again accompanied the rush of energy his mind released.

The four guards before him were violently pushed backward, hitting the wall.

He stood there confused for a half second, before running inside.

Whatever luck he lived by could run out at any moment now. He was as silent as he could be, and, following his lead, the wolves advanced softly.

Kai got to the first ship before any guards spotted him. Seeing the pack of five bluish-white wolves that reached past his shoulders get into it, Kai's mouth opened. But rather than voicing a protest they wouldn't comprehend, he shrugged and climbed further inside the dark cockpit, taking in the high-tech, unfamiliar surroundings.

He had no clue how to navigate a ship.

His uncle's voice resonated in his mind.

You know just what to do when no one explains it. Things that take years to learn, you mastered in minutes.

Ships had an autopilot, right? He just had to find a way to engage it.

"Quiet," he told the wolves, advancing toward the control panel of the ship.

It was all very complicated. A panel with a lot of options and various screens. There was a big red button on the right-hand side and a hand lever that looked important.

Who was he kidding? He couldn't do something this technical by himself. He'd never been in a spaceship before. He wasn't even familiar with the strange alphabet the instructions were written in. No way, no how.

But if he didn't somehow manage to make this thing fly, he'd die.

Kai closed his eyes. He stayed that way for a long time, too long perhaps. Any moment, the guards would find the men he'd left outside and storm the hangar....

He put that possibility, and every other worry, out of his mind and just breathed. The child found himself kneeling and holding his head down as his mind searched deep inside him.

His eyes opened again, and Kai moved to sit in the chair in front of the panel. He fastened the security belt. His arms moved like he'd done this routine a thousand times before. He would have been hard-pressed to explain what he was doing—it felt like muscle memory rather than any conscious choice. Kai started the ignition and pushed the stabilizers, then reached above his head, turning on the artificial gravity and the oxygen-level regulator. Finally, he started the engine.

The system went live. Guards shouted, pointing at him from a distance, rushing with their blasters in hand. *Shield. Activate the cloaking function, too.* He lowered the commands on his left to engage it and then activated the propulsors.

Kai was out of the hangar at high speed. He navigated out of the atmosphere before punching to warp mode, without inputting any coordinates. It didn't matter where he went, as long as it was far, far away from the only home he knew.

He briefly thought of his mother, of old Kumi, Balu, and Isha too. But still, he went forward. His life was starting now.

Kai would soon learn his bronze coin wasn't worth much in the real word. And that space could be as cold as the bitterest nights on Haimo. He felt hunger and fear and, for a long time, loneliness.

But he lived.

ENLIL, Warlord of Ratna, didn't believe in coincidences, not where magic was concerned. That he'd lose his seer, his secret weapon, the very day another mage was born in his sector meant something.

Magic didn't develop in most until later in life; children started to display these aptitudes in their teens. Yet, the Nova family reported a child who could make objects move with her mind from the cradle.

They were a good, loyal family. An old and powerful one too.

He'd had his ship prepared immediately; now he stood before the couple who ruled Itri. They looked tired. Queen Moa was as painfully beautiful as ever, and Claus, as puzzlingly undeserving of her. He was too meek for a female like his wife. She should have been consort to a male of Enlil's caliber.

Neither of them was carrying the child. They weren't even looking at her; no doubt reluctant to form an attachment for a thing destined to die.

Enlil advanced toward the servant who held the infant.

"What's her name?"

Moa closed her eyes. Claus replied, "Nalini. We called her that before...."

A good, strong name.

Enlil looked at the little thing. Unlike his own children when they'd been days old, she wasn't wiggling happily, or cooing some nonsense. She wasn't crying out either. She looked severe, as though she knew her fate was being determined.

"Three years," Enlil stated.

Moa lifted her blue eyes. Claus frowned.

"You'll keep her for three years. Make sure she can speak. I'll come for her then."

They were confused. "The Wise have decreed that mages...."

Yes, and Enlil was only too happy to carry out that directive. Mages were too powerful. A real threat to his rule.

"The Wise are hypocrites. They wield magic themselves. If it's that dangerous, why don't they jump off a cliff?"

The Novas stared at each other in shock.

"I keep one mage. She'll stay under my supervision. As long as she's loyal and useful to me, the child can live."

FOUR

THE CHILD

Nine years passed in a blink of an eye. Kai
managed just fine, most of the time. All
right, so he wasn't always on the right side
of the law. Make that never. What did they expect of
a child without a family or any friends out there? He
stole stuff to survive, making a point of only taking
from those who could afford the loss.

It had served him well until now. Today, his luck had
run out.

Damn, he hated being in chains. *Hated* it. It served as
a reminder of a past he didn't wish to ponder. Something in Kai boiled under the surface. With some
effort, he kept it under check. *No*, he told it firmly.
Never again.

It had been close to a decade since he'd made use of
that part of him, but he wasn't about to forget the

lesson he'd learned that day. Using magic wasn't a solution, not for anyone who wanted to live in peace. And where he was, in Vratis, home of the warlord of the entire Ratna Belt, it would simply have been suicide. Thieves were imprisoned; that beat what happened to mages.

Kai lifted his gaze to his hands, tied high above his head in a familiar, and uncomfortable, position. They'd used energy-field bonds, the good stuff. He wasn't going to break out of those easily. The door to his cell was flimsy in comparison, a simple lock he could pick with just about anything sharp, long, or pointy. Old-fashioned. It suited the rest of the edifice, built in the old days.

Ratna was one of the first conglomeration of systems the Evris had found when they'd left the original world they'd come from, over a thousand imperial years ago. They'd shaped it like the temples of old, with high halls and curved domes letting in light. Whoever was in charge of the decoration of the cells was old school; the structure had been modified as little as possible. Modernized, not compromised.

It said a lot about his race as a whole. So unwilling to embrace change, evolution. Stuck in the golden old days.

Kai smiled and tugged on his energy chains, observing the ceiling. Bingo. The bonds might be unrelenting, but the foundation wouldn't hold if he applied the right amount of speed and force.

He bent his knees and got ready to jump when a noise caught his attention.

Kai turned to the main doors beyond the bars of his cell, feet away. Guards. He adjusted his stance, regaining an inconspicuous position.

There were too many guards for little old Kai. At least a dozen. If he considered that they could be taking precautions because they suspected who—what—he was, he kept his concern well hidden.

One of the guards opened his cell and stepped aside to let the others pass. The rest of the guards parted, and Kai frowned in confusion.

They hadn't been here for him at all. The guards encircled someone else. A child. A boy between eight and ten years of age perhaps. His bald head drew attention to his strange eyes. Kai looked into them and felt something stir in him. Not quite fear. Not quite wariness. But there was no doubt, he needed to be careful of that child.

One of his eyes was blue, the other amber, practically gold. Both were intensely focused on him.

No. Not a boy at all, he realized. The child wore plain, asexual, simple clothing, and the lack of hair had fooled him at first, but it was a girl.

Not that it mattered. Her sex didn't change the fact that the girl was dangerous.

One humorless laugh escaped him. So much for the law everyone across the lands of Ratna diligently complied with. Their sector and the Imperials had an interesting dynamic. Everyone knew the Imperials wished they could completely claim their sector, but they didn't try. While small, the Ratna Belt was a powerful multi-planet kingdom, isolated and well protected. Still, their uneasy peace was based on the understanding that the warlord of their sector still had to obey one of their laws. Just one.

As the Wise of the Imperial Council demanded, the warlord ordered that every magic user be killed. And yet, good old Enlil kept one mage under his own roof.

Kai knew, from the bottom of his very soul, that the child was a mage. She wasn't even attempting to hide it. He felt power emanating from her. So much power.

She also knew him for what he was. Her steady, intense gaze had seen right through him, to his own essence. And she was going to tell them. That was why she'd been brought to him. No doubt, they used the child to identify and eliminate rogue mages.

«You're smarter than you look.»

He heard her voice directly in his head; her lips didn't move. Her expression remained unreadable.

"Untie him." Out loud, she sounded cold and severe, while there had been a gentleness to her tone when she'd addressed him in his mind.

No child should have quite so much authority. None of the guards thought to disobey. Seizing a control screen, one of them input his code, and the bonds disappeared.

Kai rolled his shoulders and stretched his neck.

"Thanks."

The child tilted her head. He knew his mistake right away. He'd made it sound like she'd done him a favor, perhaps even thought of his comfort. And he realized, before she even moved, that she was going to make a point of proving that she hadn't.

Her hand reached out, and violently, without so much as a warning and with no way to stop it, Kai was pushed down to his knees; his head bobbed down. Her mystical hold on him was lifted immediately. That had been a warning. Kai remained on his knees. He was right at her level that way, looking into her face.

He focused on her, trying to understand it. Her.

"What am I to search for?" she asked.

One of the guards explained, "He stole a speeder. When he was chased, he evaded our best men. We wouldn't have caught him if the owner hadn't had an infraction for unlawful parking the previous day. The vehicle was tracked."

Kai had to shake his head in distaste. Being brought down because of a parking ticket was a brand-new kind of pathetic.

"I'm not usually disturbed for petty theft," said the child.

He imagined she wasn't. No, this child probably sat next to their lord in his council chambers and spent the rest of her time meditating on the fate of the world.

He could be mistaken, but he would have sworn he saw the phantom of a thin smile on her lips for a fleeting instant.

"He was too good. Lord Enlil wants him scanned."

The child nodded before stepping toward him. She took her time. One step, then she lifted both of her hands. Another step. An intake of breath. Then, she reached out and slowly touched each side of his face. Barely. A featherlight touch.

It felt like a punch in the gut. Kai had to fight the darker part of himself harder than he ever had before. His magic wanted to lash out and recoil from those soft, warm hands.

His body stayed put. Then the real torture started.

He didn't scream. He breathed in and out, hard, in sync with the child, as vision after vision flipped through both of their minds.

Little Akai Lor of Hora crawling away from danger in the cold. Him crying that night, alone. Cursing his stars. Hunger. Darkness. Fear. Images he didn't recognize. Some he never wanted to see ever again. Others....

His mind stopped spinning, focusing on it. On her.

In this vision, Kai stood even taller than his current considerable height, and he was also older. Rougher, perhaps. He was bearing an expression that had never marred his features, yet it seemed as solid as anything he'd ever seen. He was at peace. Finally, finally at peace. And all because of her. The female in his arms smiled softly. Her sky-blue eyes looked at him as though he'd just come down from the stars and offered her the entire world.

She was the most beautiful thing he'd ever beheld, despite the scars. She had a few, none more noticeable than the raw and ugly one starting on her shoulder and running down her arm. She hadn't covered it. Tattoos had been marked on her skin around it, as if to emphasize it. There was a jewel on her forehead, as bright as her eyes.

The female was heavily pregnant. With his children, he knew. Twins. He'd call them—

The child removed her hands from Kai, taking the vision away. He practically cried out, ready to beg for more. Just another second.

That was his future. And the child was going to take it all away. She was going to turn to the guards and tell them he was a threat. A mage, and a dangerous one at that.

Kai had never been as afraid.

«*Please.*»

He implored without shame, tears in his eyes.

The child turned away from him and started walking out. He had half a second to despair.

"He's no one," said she, lying smoothly, with a carefully feigned indifference. "Just a simple, irrelevant thief."

Kai continued watching the child as her guards hurried to follow her. While someone tied his hands back toward the ceiling, still he watched her back. She left the cells without sending him one glance.

The child had lied through her teeth, he knew that. *She* knew that.

Because in the vision, he'd been wearing the warlord's robes.

FIVE
RED THREAD

Six years, three months, seven days. That's how long Nalini had spent within these walls, locked in a golden prison.

She'd learned her place early. There were servants who prepared the best foods for each of her meals, and she never had to think of washing her own robes. There were music boxes left for her amusement. Books, so many books, even on long-forgotten or forbidden subjects. Her master wanted her knowledgeable.

Still, for all her privileges, she was at the bottom of the food chain. A mouse caged in with lions. They wanted her dead. All of them. Someday, they'd get their wish.

She was a clever, tricky little mouse, though. The tigers liked watching her. As long as she did what they wanted, pretending so very hard to be one of them, to belong to their ranks, they weren't quite so willing to dispose of her. Her powers were too valuable.

So she played her part that day. Well. Very well.

She kept her face cold and expressionless. She didn't smile. She didn't even cry. She didn't fall to her knees and ask why these burdens fell on her small shoulders.

Kai, he was called. Akai Lor, son of Hora. Bastard. Mage. Monster.

Someday, he'd burn this world down. He'd tear down the skies. The reach of his darkness was limitless.

No, that wasn't quite right. If she'd only seen that, she would have killed him herself with one wave of her hand. She could, now. He wasn't yet in control of his devastating powers.

She hadn't even considered ending him, because there was so much more in Kai. An equal potential for good. He could, and even might, bring peace to their worlds, forever destroying the rift between mages and the other Evris. He was the key to their destruction, or their salvation. From her confusing waves of visions, each outcome seemed as likely right now. He hadn't marked his fate in stone yet.

Ultimately, she'd decided it wasn't up to her, a child

who knew but little of these things, to dictate his fate. It all felt so much bigger than her.

There was another thing. A selfish motive. She was reluctant to admit it, even to herself.

Nalini Nova returned to her chambers and sat on her meditation mat, smiling to herself. He'd seen that, clearly visualizing her sitting, legs crossed, in this very room.

She closed her eyes and searched for an answer, exploring as much of the future, and the past, as her power allowed her to see. Nothing new, no magic answer, came to her, but now she'd taken a minute to think and calm down, her resolve was firm.

When she opened her eyes again, both were gold.

She closed her fists. In another part of the castle, down in the dungeon, Kai fell to the ground, his energy bonds undone. Nalini tilted her head. A click resounded as his cell opened. She then lifted her hand, focusing so hard, beads of sweat gathered on her forehead.

«*The guards on your left are asleep*», she told him.

Kai remained where he stood, eyes widened in surprise.

«*I won't hold this for long.*»

Another second passed, then, deciding she wasn't trying to trick him, he ran along the left corridor.

«*Wait,*» she said.

The recording devices set up to observe the palace worked continuously, but the screens of the guards in charge of watching them changed periodically.

«*Now,*» said she, when the guards started to monitor another area. «*There are spare uniforms on your right. Take the plain green one.*»

Janitor. No one would look twice at him in that get-up.

«*You have two minutes. Get changed and take the service elevator down to the gardens. Look down. Good luck.*»

She was reluctant to let go of the connection. Right when she was about to cut it, he said, «*You're a prisoner here.*» It wasn't a question, and she needn't answer it.

«*Come with me.*»

She almost laughed. The warlord wouldn't think much of an irrelevant thief breaking out of his dungeon, but if *she* disappeared? He'd burn down cities to find her.

«*There's a tracker inside me*», she told him.

A pause. «*I'll come back,* Kai replied. «*I'll come back and get you out of here. I owe you, little lady.*»

This time, Nalini broke the link without a second of hesitation.

That he'd come back to Vratis someday was a fact. But would it be for her, or would it be to clench his insatiable thirst for power?

She knew exactly what had started that day. On her bookshelves behind her, a dozen books spoke of it. All of those were forbidden to common folks. The Wise had dictated that they should remain unaware of it, to avoid panic and confusion.

There was a reason why Evris killed those amongst them who displayed an aptitude for magic. There was a reason why she was watched and controlled. She needed to be. Her kind was dangerous. Her kind could bring an end to thousands of worlds. They almost did once.

A prophecy written twelve hundred years ago — back before the Evris had ever left Tejen, their original world — spoke of it happening again. It spoke of a mage of great power and great darkness, rising from the ashes, born in shame and who'd one day kill their Goddess Light.

It spoke of the evil lord who could create Starfire, the single most deadly energy source.

It spoke of a monster. And she'd just saved his life.

NALINI CARRIED on moving her hands aimlessly, stretching and training her body. There was nothing strange in her actions. Those who would, no doubt, watch the recording closely after Kai's escape wouldn't find anything unusual.

Still, she'd be chastised. The warlord would demand to know why she hadn't seen the escape. He would question her answers, wondering if she was quite as loyal as she seemed. He would tighten his grasp on her in the next years, until the ultimate, unavoidable climax.

Her own future was often clouded to her. She couldn't see all of this quite clearly, but she could imagine it. She dreaded it. Yet, something in her whispered two words.

Worth it.

Even as she took her punishment later, she didn't regret her actions.

The warlord loved his machines. His favorite one was the cage he locked her in. He sent pulses of energy through it, shocking her mind and body so hard she screamed.

Training, he called it. If she wasn't strong enough to

fight against an insignificant thief, no doubt she needed it.

Her instructions were simple. *Resist it. Block it.*

He had his men set the blasts to their highest strength that day. There was no resisting it. There was just pain, meant to break her body and her spirit.

She took the pain in and remained unscratched where it mattered, those two words etched in her very psyche.

It had been worth it. If only to see Enlil's world burn one day.

Everything in Kai protested against his steps. Told him to turn back and go get the kid. The strange little lady might have gotten herself in some trouble when she chose to help him.

Such concern for a near stranger was quite uncharacteristic of him. He wasn't what one would call selfless. But that child had changed something deep inside him. He couldn't exactly figure out how.

He thought about her. Her ordeal in that cold palace, the way she'd had to grow up fast to survive. And, by extension, Kai considered the rest of his kind. Their kind.

There were mages in this world, the rest of the sector, and all around the galaxy. Mages who died chained up and left to the wolves. Others who reached adulthood, but had to constantly survive in fear and hide who they were, like him.

He'd always known that, but whenever he'd thought of any of them, he'd purposefully put it out of his mind. It wasn't like he could do anything about them, right? Or so he'd told himself, before seeing a freaking child fight in the middle of their enemy's home, in silence, without expecting any reward or recognition for her effort. Taking risks for no other reason than the fact that it was the right thing to do.

Kai turned away from the palace. Getting caught again in an attempt to break the girl out wasn't a solution. It wouldn't solve the core of the problem. He took the longest way back to his current hideout, as though purposefully wanting to pass through the poorest, dirtiest districts of Vratis, to convince himself he was making the right decision.

There was a boy too hungry to cry or beg, just sitting there with his hand outstretched. Kai didn't have anything to give him. And whatever he could have spared wouldn't have helped in the long run. Thus was their world. Golden palaces and famine living side by side, hand in hand.

By the time he'd made it to his ship, the Kai who'd run at nine years old and spent the second half of his life aimlessly traveling their sector, taking what he wanted, living without rules, was dead. Buried by the male he was always meant to become. Murdered by a little lady whose name he didn't know yet.

A large beast jumped up to him, putting her paws on his shoulders, and flapping her tail. Sky.

"I'm alright, girl."

The wolf inspected him herself, and licked his face before putting her front paws back on the floor, satisfied.

They walked side by side into the ship. As soon as they'd passed the trapdoor, his first and only partner greeted him with a grumble. "I heard you'd been snatched."

Kai lifted a brow. "And yet, you're still here, with my ship."

Ian Krane was a grumpy old male. Kai'd ended up saddled with him because they'd attempted to steal the same ship a few years back.

"She's mine," Krane immediately protested.

"I am the person sitting in the captain's chair. By definition, that makes it my ship."

They had this particular argument on a weekly basis. Technically, the ship belonged to both of them. They'd shared everything equally since they'd teamed up, and they'd both put the money down to get this custom, modified beauty made for them.

"Only because these damn beasts don't let me anywhere near it," he replied. "Doesn't change the fact that my name is on the papers."

Krane did love to complain—about anything and everything. Especially the four other wolves now coming to greet Kai. Never mind the fact that the old male was, more often than not, stroking one of them right between the ears.

Kai smiled. If anyone had asked him, he would have said he put up with Ian Krane because most heists were easier to pull off with a partner, and flying the Zonian with a copilot made sense. But he might end up missing Krane, now that it was time to part ways.

"Listen, I'm gonna change direction a bit." A lot. "I mean, we have plenty of money."

Krane watched him carefully.

"You're not going regular on me, are you?"

Kai laughed, imagining working behind a desk or opening a shop. Yeah, not for him. "No. Quite the opposite."

The older male waited. "I was caught," Kai confirmed. "And I had help. I got lucky." The word didn't sit well with him. Meeting that child hadn't quite felt like something as casual and mundane as luck. "Anyway, I just saw that our system is sick at the core today. On one side you have cold, hunger, slavery, and then the other, with the fat, indulgent nobles who feed off of it." After a beat, he added quietly, "There are children killed because they develop abilities that frighten those in power."

Krane watched him intently. Then, he laughed.

"Color me surprised. Kai, who refuses to work for nobles, refuses to pay their taxes, always steals from them and no one else, revealing that he's anti-government." He rolled his eyes. "That ain't nothing new."

He shrugged. "Maybe not. Except maybe now I want to do something about it."

The old man's keen, green eyes sparkled. "And about time, too, kiddo. About time."

ENLIL WATCHED THE RECORDING, lips thin. They were right. The boy had used magic.

"And Nalini scanned him, you said?" he asked the head of his guard, who bobbed his head.

"Yes, not even an hour before."

Hmm.

He watched a hologram showing the entire interrogation, careful to scrutinize Nalini's expression. The child remained stoic as ever. Cold and cruel, as she generally was with enemies. She'd been that way at three years of age, why would she be any different at nine? Then, he watched her leave and go to her room. Surveillance drones trailed her every step.

She was training, something she did often. She stretched first and then she started with her various weapons.

None of his mages had ever displayed an interest in the art of war. Nalini had asked to be taught how to fight at age five. "I want to defend myself in case enemies get to me," she'd said. Enlil agreed she should learn. He'd assumed she'd be as interested in these things as his own daughter, who had picked up fencing and given it up within one imperial year, but four years later, the child still persevered. She wasn't half bad. He'd had a tracker placed inside her the previous year, just in case.

Enlil observed her with her baton. Precise and fast, not very strong, though. She wasn't allowed a real sword; the warlord didn't feel comfortable having her armed with steel. The child was already dangerous. Too dangerous, perhaps. Had she ever displayed any belligerence, he would have been forced to dispose of her.

Perhaps he should, regardless, but Enlil wasn't fond of the idea of doing without such a powerful weapon.

His power had considerably increased since he'd taken the child in. His rule of the Ratna Belt had been conditional on the Imperials' approval until recently. As their sector was on the outer border, not quite part of the imperial territory, they were mostly left alone. But when the Imperials required their resources, they demanded them, and paid a pittance, too. With Nalini's foresight abilities, which were always accurate, he'd led an embarrassingly short battle against one young, impetuous Imperial commander.

The boy's considerable loss had made it clear to every Imperial lying in wait that Ratnarians were no pushovers and asserted Enlil's dominion.

The girl could foresee the outcome of wars, but she hadn't seen that a young boy was going to escape? Or that he had magic himself?

Enlil frowned. Nalini had only showed loyalty until now. But this was one offense he couldn't just brush away. Not when the child was so powerful.

"Put her under *constant* observation," he ordered. "Not just drones. I want one guard to have eyes on her at all times. If she acts out of character, notify me immediately."

His gaze returned to the hologram of the boy. Or young male, perhaps. If he'd really thwarted Nalini's probing, he was dangerous.

"And put a damn bounty on that boy."

"How much?" asked his private secretary.

"A hundred."

That amount would steadily rise over the next few years, as the unidentified thief continued evading them. But it was nothing compared to the millions of marks he would offer for any information that could lead to the capture of the magic user he would come to know as Kai Lor.

SEVEN
THE LOTUS

K ai hadn't believed he'd ever let go of the Zonian, the large freighter he'd called his for the best part of a decade.

Each of his wolves had their respective cabin, Krane slept on his copilot chair, and Kai's small apartment was the closest thing he'd ever had to an actual safe home. One bed, just long and broad enough for his frame. Shelves atop of it; their contents would have fallen right on his face at the slightest turbulence. That didn't bother him; if there was turbulence, he certainly didn't want to sleep through it.

Sky slept at his feet. The five wolves who'd left Haimo with him were as far from domesticated as any animal could be. They followed him around because they'd decided he was pack—their alpha, to be precise. Sky had been the alpha before him. For a time, Kai had wondered whether the beast was following him around to catch him at a disadvantage someday. Rip his throat out and reclaim her title. But, in time, he'd learned to sleep in her presence. Now, he couldn't sleep at all without feeling her there.

This was truly home. An old male and five beasts in a modified ship full of stolen goods.

But whatever way he thought of it, he needed to let her go. His plan depended on it. He had to have a new ship.

"You'll have to pilot her," Kai stated reluctantly. He just couldn't see another way.

Krane scratched his head. "Hmm. Yeah, you'll need something smaller, less conspicuous, too. I guess we're in the market for a light fighter."

Kai nodded stiffly; the very notion was distasteful to him. He wasn't much different from the wolves—a den animal, protective of its territory.

Half an hour into his tour of the closest tech sector, he had a change of heart.

Kai had no clue how Krane had managed to get them onto Tor Koa, a tightly guarded imperial planet, given the fact that they were both wanted outlaws, but there they were, being shown around by an elegant, well-dressed noble who was talking to them like they were valued customers.

Not for the first time, Kai wondered who exactly *was* old Ian Krane.

Then he was too busy drooling over the designs their host was showcasing to think about it too much.

"This one is a beauty," Wen Aris, their host, told him, catching sight of the slender, silver ship he couldn't stop watching. "She'll be available commercially next year. But she's in working order. Her Highness made it clear that any model you require will be available for your use."

Again, Kai turned to Krane, who seemed quite fascinated with his nails right then.

So, he *did* have some noble contacts, and amongst the Imperials, no less.

Kai let it go. He certainly had his own private history, and he wouldn't have appreciated it if his companion had started digging into it.

"She's a Battria-X7 model. Designed for speed and protection. Her cannons and front blasters are lethal, like the X6, but, what makes her special, along with a velocity of point six past lightspeed in warp mode, is her shields. As resilient as those of most cargo and command ships. She'll be the safest light transport in the market once we start selling her."

Kai didn't even consciously move his hand, yet it was extended, almost caressing the window separating him from the ship. Their Zonian was fast, no doubt about it, but no freighter of her size could go above point three past lightspeed. Smaller, slimmer, with modern materials, the light spaceship models they watched now went twice as fast.

"What do you think, kiddo?"

He had trouble putting what he thought into words.

"She won't be cheap."

The old male just laughed it off. "It's on me. I can keep the Zonian and get you this baby as payment for your half of it."

Only, a thousand Zonians wouldn't have amounted to the price tag of *this* technological beauty.

"Don't sweat it, boy. Someone owes me a favor. I'm collecting. No money will exchange hands on this."

Kai recalled getting small, insignificant presents on a yearly basis. A small scarf with his name embroidered on it. A toy. A little knife. It had been a long, long time ago. He hadn't thought he'd ever feel that way again.

"The wolves can't live in there. She's too small."

Ian shrugged off his concern.

"They can stay with me when you're using her." He turned to the noble. "Does it come in black?"

Wen nodded with grace. "All our ships are entirely customizable."

"Good, good. Let's get the details sorted." They started walking away, speaking low, whispering secrets Kai chose not to intrude on. Besides, he was too busy drooling over the ship, checking out its every angle.

"Kai!" Ian called out at some point. "What's her name?"

He should have thought about it long and hard. Naming a ship was no small matter; it had taken them a long time to settle on the Zonian years ago.

But eyes flashed through Kai's mind. One blue, one gold. He just said, "Lotus." Why the child made him think of a lotus at all, he wasn't sure. But calling his ship after the little lady who'd saved his life felt right. "The Black Lotus."

"I like it. Classy. Slightly evil. Suits you."

And she did.

HIS FIRST MISSION was badly planned and should have ended up in a disaster. The Lotus saved his damn skin though. Wen Aris was no liar, evidently; her shields were worth their weight in gold.

Kai and Krane used to listen to the authorities' communications to avoid them; now, catching their frequencies, they intercepted words about a kid accused of weilding magic. Kai knew he had to at least try to do something about it.

"We're not ready," Krane said. Rightly so.

Kai nodded. "There are only regular guards posted. The inquisitors said they'd be in in the morning. They don't expect anyone to drop in and try to break the kid out."

That, he knew from experience.

Krane sighed and just told him, "Don't die," knowing he had no way of dissuading Kai from doing anything he wanted to do.

Kai boarded the Lotus, his brand-new, just delivered, Lotus. At Krane's demand, it was painted black, with red engines and propulsors, which only served to make her more gorgeous.

Sky approved.

"You're not supposed to be in there," he told the wolf, who thoroughly ignored him, stubbornly remaining planted on his heels.

Kai sighed and started the engine. Krane opened the trapdoor under the Zonian to let her out.

EIGHT
IN THE BEGINNING

Essel was a small planet of little relevance, other than its physical proximity to Vratis.; it was one of the planets directly under the control of the warlord, simply because it was situated in the same system as his ruling city. The child with magic had been found in one of the farisles, off the planet's southern hemisphere, but when the reports had come in, the authorities had brought him to the main city.

After landing, Kai made his way to a small pub he knew, where the ale flowed freely and tongues ran just as easily. He got the whole story within half an hour.

The prison wasn't well secured, thankfully. Just a dozen guards, some of them chilling in their break room, others playing chess.

It should have been easy. It wasn't.

Walking into a prison didn't require any particular skills; walking out with someone you're not meant to take with you could prove problematic, he'd soon learn.

Kai was lucky enough to start with. The official at the reception desk was particularly dense.

"Hey, do you mind if I fill out an application form? Always wanted to wear one of your exosuits."

The soldier puffed his chest. "There's a little more to being an enforcer than wearing a cool exosuit," he said, all the while opening a drawer and fetching an application form.

He had *really* fallen for it? Kai stared, speechless. Who actually *wanted* to be an enforcer?

He observed the area behind the reception desk as the guard was distracted. A light control panel. New tech flap doors, no doubt set to only open to authorized personnel. Cameras. Floating surveillance drones.

He bit his lip.

"There you go."

Kai took the pile of forms and the pen the guard helpfully handed him, before walking away.

What now?

He thought back to his own stay in the warlord's prison. The child had reached into his mind and talked to him. She'd knocked out the guards. Damn, she'd be handy right about then. Still, he might not be able to do anything like that, but he had other skills.

Kai discreetly slid a command control down his sleeve and placed it atop his pile of papers. He began entering codes, typing so fast the screen blurred.

He smirked. The security around their server was downright laughable. The lights, along with every other machine in the building, shut off.

"What was that?"

He smirked as the buffoon behind the desk got to his feet, looking around. "No clue, mate. A bad fuse?"

"Maybe. Let me call someone."

"Sure. I'll stay right here," Kai lied. The second he'd disappeared, Kai got to his feet and made his way toward the back of the precinct.

Turned out, quiet, irrelevant planet or not, they were busy in Essel. Almost every cell was occupied with at least two or three inmates, all of whom cheered and called to him. Kai ran through the long corridors, looking over his shoulder, expecting guards to be alerted by the commotion any second.

He found the child in the last cell. There was no doubt that it was the boy he sought; no child of twelve or thirteen would have been imprisoned for any reason but magic. Besides, the boy watched him with resigned eyes, not even crying in fear.

He knew that look. This was a mage living on borrowed time.

"Hey, look, I'm here to get you out, okay?"

The boy's expression was shocked, more than anything else.

Kai didn't have time to try to convince him. He was locked away behind a console meant to be opened with fingerprint identification.

"Shit," he cursed, hearing fast footsteps behind him, approaching at high speed. "Okay, step away from the doors."

The boy obeyed carefully.

"Here goes nothing...."

Kai hadn't used magic in so long, he didn't even know if he still could. But the moment he decided to, the moment he breathed, just breathed and reached down inside, he found it.

Just like he had years ago, his hand reached out as he called to the energy around him and used it, firing directly at the cage. The console exploded, pushing the door off its hinges. Every other door in the entire precinct opened, as well.

Good thing. The guards were going to be busy.

Right then, the lights turned back on and a high-pitched alarm resounded through the building.

"You're okay?" he asked the stunned kid who looked at him like he'd grown horns and a tail over the course of the last half second.

"You're a mage."

He was, although it now seemed like a strange fact, too long ignored.

"So are you, I hear."

The boy nodded, his expression terrified at the very prospect.

Kai wanted to tell him it was no big deal, that his ability to use energy didn't define what kind of person he was. But even if he had been any good at sharing feelings, they didn't exactly have the time for a heart to heart, so he simply said, "Let's get out of here."

But that proved to be difficult, with every exit blocked and more guards surrounding the building at every instant.

They found a service staircase; he considered going down to get out, but figured any male called in would arrive that way. Instead, they headed up to the roof. A bad idea. Second mental note: prisons generally had a security droid posted on their roof, and when they were on alert, they also had fighting drones firing away. Kai grabbed the kid up and danced away to avoid the blasts coming at them from all sides. Good thing the machines weren't that great at aiming. That, or he wasn't bad at avoiding their shots.

Finally, there she came. The red lights of his beautiful *Lotus*, heading toward him thanks to the beacon he wore on his wrist. The ship was so responsive, she could practically think. It started firing at the drones, which turned their attention to her, rather than carrying on trying to kill Kai and the boy.

"Listen, what's your name, kid?"

"Wench," the teenager replied. He shrugged. "I'm small. Pa says I should have been a girl, so he calls me Wench."

Fucking stupid father. "Right. Well, how good are you at jumping?"

"Errr...."

"If it's jumping or dying."

"Pretty good. I'm pretty good at not dying."

Clever boy. Kai dropped him at his side, grabbed his arm, and they ran hard to gain some momentum, then they jumped together toward the boarding platform and open trapdoor underneath the Lotus. The ship closed the entrance as soon as they were safely inside.

Kai couldn't believe they'd somehow gotten in there without getting shot, given his poor-ass plan.

"Get us out of here," he ordered. The ship acknowledged the voice control and sped away from the danger at high speed.

Sky awaited him, lying down next to the captain's chair. He could have sworn the wolf was shaking her head at him. Still, she licked his hand when he passed her by.

"Wow," the boy named Wench mused. "That was literally insane. And have you *seen* this ship?"

"Trust me, I have."

"And is that a *wolf*?"

Boys. Kai managed a thin smile; everything seemed to delight the impressionable teenager.

"Meet Sky. Touch her at your own risk."

The she-wolf bared her teeth to punctuate that statement. Wench didn't take it personally, too busy looking everywhere in wonder.

"This ship is going to be wanted throughout the galaxy after today," the boy said, and Kai nodded.

"Yep. Which is why we aren't flying her through the galaxy." He pointed to the small freighter now coming into view. "The Zonian. She's pretty plain and easily cloaked."

"And no one will think that you're hiding a freaking beauty like this inside *that* old dumpster."

Kai glared.

"Call her that again and you'll *walk*."

No one insulted his ship. Or Krane's, anyway.

The old male and four wolves were waiting for them when they got back.

"You managed, then."

He inclined his head. "Only just."

The male nodded. "We'll be better prepared next time."

And they were. The next time and the time after that.

After a few months, Kai started to wonder what he was supposed to do with the dozens of teenagers and slightly younger boys and girls who now inhabited the Zonian. There was just enough room for them, and every month, their numbers rose. Soon, the ship would be crowded.

That's when the first of them turned up. An adult, actually older than Kai. He'd heard about a rogue who risked his skin to save mage kids.

"I thought it was just talk at first. Legends. But

someone I trust swore it was happening. I knew it was time."

Lawer was a transporter specializing in high-risk cargo, legal or illegal. He also was a mage who'd managed to hide it for longer than Kai.

He wasn't the only one who sought him out.

A year later, Kai had a fleet. Seven larger ships, three dozen fighters. A small fleet, but a fleet nonetheless. There was no other word for it.

That's when he took over his first planet, in the year 1214—almost by accident.

NINE

ALLIANCES

Nalini never lost track of Kai.

It took a while for her to identify their strange link, the life force she was somehow always conscious of; it felt far and close all at once. Each time she cleared her mind and meditated, under the order of Warlord Enlil, to scan for relevant threats, she felt it. Him.

She was twelve when she consciously realized what it was. Over the course of the three previous years, it had been a familiar, yet foreign, presence she somehow got used to. It bothered her at first, but after months, she'd come to terms with the fact that she couldn't cut it out or shield herself away from it. And later, she'd learned to find comfort in that familiar presence that made her feel a little less alone in her darkest nights.

She learned it was Kai the day he almost died. The usually benign, inconsequential awareness made itself pressing, almost painful. She knew what to do instinctively, as though something else—someone else —deep inside her had done it a thousand times.

She closed her eyes, letting her body collapse where it stood, although she'd been in a meeting. Poor Enlil made a fuss over her after the fainting spell. He'd insisted that she had to take more fresh air and fed her nice fresh fruits for weeks after that. He'd grown so very fond of his favorite weapon, losing it to sickness wouldn't sit well with him.

As her shell fell, her consciousness travelled at an impossible speed, pulling her where she needed to be.

Kai was sitting on a plain single bed. He'd changed in three years; unlike her, he was quite grown up. He wore white clothing and, over it, a grayish sort of cape. And there was something in his expression she hadn't seen before. Something darker, wilder.

"You!"

He saw her. She lifted a brow, startled and confused.

"Me," she confirmed, turning on her heels to observe their surroundings, trying to understand what was happening.

They were in a small chamber that was kept neat,

clothing folded and piled up on a shelf, the bed was made, and there was a blaster at the ready next to the pillow. Good.

"What are you doing here?"

An interesting question. Not sure how to answer it, she countered with one of her own. "Where are we?"

He observed her closely, frowning.

"Tenera, in the Krazu system," he practically growled. "The royals make children fight in a pit for their amusement around these parts."

The very idea seemed repulsive to him. She smiled, hoping against all hope that he'd stay that way. That he'd stay good.

There was a chance he wouldn't. Someday, he might be a new Enlil. Only much, much more powerful. Part of her knew to fear him for that possibility.

"You've infiltrated them in order to attempt to break them out," she guessed, impressed and a little proud, too.

Kai nodded.

"Well, I'm pretty sure you were found out. You're about to die," she told him, because she felt it at the core of her very being.

As a seer, she knew better than to ignore her instincts.

"Are you serious?"

She nodded. "And now that I'm here, I might just die along with you."

A guess, but now that she'd said it, it felt right. To test a theory, she brought her fingers close to the nearest object—a chair. She wasn't surprised when her skin touched the metallic surface, finding it cold.

"I'm really here," she mused.

Nalini felt the presence before they heard a dozen footsteps speeding their way.

"I hope you're good with that." She waved toward his blaster, which briskly flew out toward him; Kai jumped to his feet, caught it, and raised it rather than asking questions. He trusted her implicitly, she realized, stunned because she wasn't used to it. Enlil doubted her every word, questioning her motives. He demanded every detail, every reasoning, before settling on a course of action.

When the door slid open, Kai undid the safety and shot without hesitation. Good thing, too; the intruders had come armed, no doubt intending to catch him by surprise. That's how he would have died, Nalini guessed.

One male fell, the second raised his weapon; she didn't give him the time to shoot, tightening her fist and twisting it, breaking his neck. A neat trick she couldn't do often; it took focus and her hold had to last for several seconds, which rendered that skill useless in an actual fight, when things moved so fast. Now that the ten official enforcers dressed in black and red had noticed her, she didn't have that luxury.

Fortunately, Kai's shots were lethal. The enforcers had noticed as much; they took cover on either side of the door, shooting blindly into the room.

Kai waved their way leisurely, and an energy wall erected, protecting them from the blasts. He hadn't just changed physically; he was more powerful now.

Much more powerful.

Part of her wanted to take a careful step back. She wasn't familiar with the feeling of finding herself in the company of someone whose mind was as strong as hers.

What if *he* became her enemy? What then? Could she defend herself from him? Possibly, now. But she'd spent twelve years learning just how she could control and manipulate the energy around her, training, one energy blast after the next in that cage. Other ways, too. Kai started to explore it three years ago. In another few years, he might surpass her. Have the ability to crush her.

"I can't hold that forever, and they'll soon realize their technique is useless. You have to get out of here."

He was thinking of her safety. He wasn't a threat to her. Not now. Possibly not ever. Her one action that day, years ago, might have earned his loyalty—something he didn't bestow easily.

This was guesswork. With most, Nalini would have simply scanned their mind and intentions. With him, she couldn't. He kept her out completely, and effortlessly.

"I can't." That wasn't quite true; now that the immediate danger had passed, she felt like, if she let go, calmed down, and concentrated on getting back to her body, she *could*. But there was just one problem with that. "They've seen me. If they report my presence, I'm dead. I need to...."

Those two nasty words wouldn't cross her lips. *Kill them.* End a life. She'd done it a moment ago, but stopping to think of it made her nauseous.

Still, there was no other choice. Her looks were too unusual; if they talked to anyone of importance of a young girl with eyes of a different color, a bald head, and beige clothing that would befit a monk, she'd be identified immediately. Enlil would have her chamber gassed in the middle of the night, killing her in her sleep.

Not needing her to elaborate, Kai nodded before launching out of the room. She followed.

When he discarded his blaster, she wondered why

for a second; then he pulled two strange weapons—rounded disk knives—out of the back of his coat and slashed through arms and throats at the speed of a tornado.

She got it. He fought with the precision of an artist and the ferocity of a wild beast; blasters probably slowed him down. Nalini stared openmouthed until she felt one of the enforcer's intention. A blaster, aimed at Kai's back. She moved instinctively.

It was the first time she actually fought, really physically fought, against an adversary who'd destroy her if he could. Until then, she'd simply trained by herself, or sparred with fighting masters who treated her like a porcelain doll.

She realized just how weak her little arms were. Just how hard a kick to the stomach felt. But still, she held her own against simple Teneran law enforcers. Her power helped. She kicked one male in the head and took his baton as he fell forward; using the metal weapon, she bashed through bones with speed and purpose. Her muscles might be puny, but backed up by her mind's compulsion, her blows were deadly.

The entire fight didn't last more than four minutes; then Nalini and Kai stood—him unscratched, her, winded and a little bruised, but fine.

He seemed impressed. "Not bad, little lady."

She huffed a nervous laugh, all the while looking

around the corridor's ceiling. It didn't look like there was a camera.

"I could say the same." He'd taken out seven of the guys, leaving her just three.

"First time I had someone guarding my back," he confessed, bending down to retrieve his blaster. "Could get used to it."

"Let's try not to do this again, instead," Nalini replied, rolling her eyes. "*Ever.*"

"Why *are* we doing this? Why are you here?" So much for not being the type to ask questions. Apparently, he was just the type of guy who saved them for when he wasn't about to die. She frowned.

"Not sure." She shrugged to emphasize her ignorance and innocence in the matter. "I guess the cosmos doesn't want me to let you die, or something."

He looked at her for a long time, his dark gaze intense. Finally, he inclined his head, accepting that response.

"I owe you, either way. Again."

"We'll keep a tab. You can repay me with interest."

Kai smiled. "Cute."

She rolled her eyes.

"You've grown up," he remarked, sizing her up. "How old are you now?"

"Twelve."

He nodded. "And you're still a prisoner. You're not really here; I can't smell or feel your presence."

Nalini nodded.

"I'll really get you out, someday."

"Unlikely."

He frowned.

"I need to go."

But his intense dark eyes kept her in place, scrutinizing her in a way that made her feel strange, more self-conscious than she was with dozens of drones constantly set on her.

"Right," he sounded reluctant. "Until next time then."

She bobbed her head before letting go of the link she was holding on to. She felt light, lighter than air.

"Wait," Kai called out. "What's your name?"

She could have answered, but Nalini chose to say something else before she disappeared.

"Wear a mask. Your face is on record."

That seemed more important than anything else.

When she felt the presence again, the day after, and the day after that, she knew exactly who she was linked to. She felt it when he got hurt and, once or twice, pushed some of her own energy through their bond to allow him to heal faster.

Nalini might have gone insane within the five following years if it hadn't been for that bond.

Then, that day she'd seen so long ago finally came.

TEN
PEACE

Now alone, Kai remained immobile and confused for a beat, before he forced himself into moving. He had a mission. Now that he'd been compromised, he needed to get down there and break the kids out before it was too late.

There was no time for subtlety. He was alone, without backup; Kai made his way through the Teneran palace, slicing through or incapacitating anyone who crossed his path armed with a blaster.

He'd never been quite so confident, not even questioning whether he was going to survive this. There were hundreds of enemies, all alerted to his presence, all heading toward him, and he just walked through, destroying them one by one.

No need to wonder why: the little lady had done this. Changed something fundamental in him again.

The kid was a seer. The visions he'd seen through her eyes had made that clear. She'd appeared because he'd been about to die, and she'd only left because he was safe now. With that knowledge in mind, he felt invincible. It was as though she was right there, behind him, watching over him.

Kai unfolded another layer of his power, so suddenly it was almost painful. He moved instinctively, avoiding shots before they were even fired. Every day for over a year, he'd become a little stronger, pushing his abilities one step further at a time, tentatively testing his limits. Finally, he understood. There were no limits. That power didn't belong to him, wasn't born inside him. He simply borrowed it from the universe around him, the energy binding and linking all things. The infinity. He could channel the girl from three worlds away simply because they were part of the same universe.

The moment he accepted this truth, every single soul awake in the city of Rumaul, homestead of Tenera, fell unconscious.

Kai's soul aged a decade in a few milliseconds, suddenly taking in the weight of such knowledge, an understanding of the universe only the most ancients of the Wise shared with him.

Them and a little girl on Vratis.

Finding his footing, he ran down to the arena. The uncommon sight before his eyes had him raising a brow.

He activated the comm device at his wrist. "Going to need some help down here," he told his command shuttle.

"Copy that. Division coming through."

His men arrived just as startled as he'd been at first, finding hundreds of soldiers still unconscious. The children were also in their cells, now wide open.

"Wait, so what did you call us for?" Lawer mused.

Kai shrugged, a rare cocky smile on his lips.

"Can't carry them all by myself."

His men watched him with expressions ranging from awe to fear. He ignored it.

"Wait," said Hart.

The twenty-year-old, well-bred male didn't mind getting his hands dirty, helping out in fights when he was needed, but his real strength lay between his ears. He – and his twin sister – were smart. Their parents were politicians, and they'd taught them to think, use their brains when everyone else just did the obvious thing.

When Hart spoke, they all listened.

"We don't actually need to get the kids out."

Kai lifted a questioning brow.

"Everyone is out for the count, right? Every single soldier in the place."

He nodded slowly.

"So how about we get *them* in cells? The droids and war machines can be reprogrammed. And we can stay here."

The idea had merit. Kai pondered it seriously. Their fleet almost never touched ground, as they were in danger as soon as they arrived in any known system. They fueled up, stocked up on resources, and went back out in space. It would be nice to have a base of sorts.

In fact, if they took Tenera, they could stay there. Just defend it, and let it be known that it was a safe haven for those wielding magic.

"Right."

They did just that.

It had been an idealistic dream, an illusion that didn't last.

Magic users came in numbers—men and women, children of all ages. Evris with no magic came too, simply enticed by the idea of a world Enlil didn't control. Many souls, on every world, seemed to have waited for this time, hoping that it would come someday.

Kai was humbled and encouraged when he saw that they numbered in the thousands. Tens of thousands.

THEY WERE ATTACKED by the warlord's fleet within weeks.

Ian Krane laughed. "I told you it wasn't going to be that easy."

True, the old grouch, always the naysayer, had warned him not to get too comfortable. Still, Rumaul had been built to withstand a siege, giving them an advantage: while the enemy fleet could attack in space, it couldn't blow up the city. They erected an energy shield no weapon could pierce from the outside, before jumping into every single available fighter. Kai allowed every boy and girl of age to defend their new home if they so wished, and ensured that his best soldiers remained behind, to take care of those who were too young to fight yet.

"I can help!" Wench yelled stubbornly when he was denied the chance to jump into a fighter.

The boy was fourteen, and already a good pilot, but

he was still too inexperienced for battle. Too young to kill.

Kai sighed, recalling the existence of a twelve-year-old with strange eyes, who simply had to click her finer to kill grown males. So, perhaps it was a poor excuse. Age had little to do with anything in war. But Wench wasn't ready, and Kai wouldn't have his blood on his hands.

"You can help," Kai nodded, knowing what kind of person he'd been at fourteen. Already self-sufficient and old enough to do just about everything himself. Wench had never been put in a situation where he had to be 100 percent in charge of his own fate, like Kai had in his youth, but they certainly weren't coddling him like mother hens. He'd be just as useful as any other pair of hands. His mind raced, and finally, Kai knew just what to do with him. "Go down to mechanics. Make sure the damn shield stays in place. Whatever it takes, boy."

There were a dozen men down in the control room, tending to that shield, but now that he'd been given a purpose that didn't require him staying planted on his butt and twiddling his thumbs, Wench nodded and went on his way.

Kai got to the Lotus.

That's when the fight was over, really.

That ship. That beautiful, beautiful ship.

Kai's flying had always been responsive, instinctive, and the Lotus's system was built to anticipate his next intention before he'd finished a maneuver. Moves that would have been entirely impossible in any ship half its size, were seamless.

Kai spun at high speed, shooting to take out the two main canons of the Lordship, their enemy's main command ship, one after the other.

"Leader to all light fighters," Kai called, "stay with me on this one. I need all fire on their command platform."

"Their shield is still up," one of his fighters pointed out. "No way can we pierce that with our—"

Well, simple requests, simple answers. "I'll take the shield out. Over."

Kai got the Lotus to scan the Lordship's configuration. It might be a custom design, but it had been based on a larger scale TX-999; he'd studied that model to decide whether it was worth stealing a while back. Their controls were all safely tucked underneath the main body of the ship, protected between the now-disabled canons.

Kai shot at the platform repetitively. When that failed, he lifted his hand and concentrated, straining hard. This wasn't like knocking out a weak-minded Evris or blasting a door. Magic was simply another word for manipulating energy without the assistance of any technology—using just his mind. And the shield he went against *was* made of energy.

He needed help. The instant he realized that, he knew who to ask.

A little lady.

Her eyes flashed through his mind. He felt her watching him, assessing the situation. Almost immediately, an excess of power blasted through, so strong and sudden, he felt faint.

Kai yelled in pain and drops of blood dripped from his nose. Before his eyes, the brightly lit command ship with purple propulsors went dark, then lit back up with dim, dull lighting. Kai's control panel showed practically no energy coming from the Lordship now. Fuck. The force he'd released hadn't just taken out the Lordship's shields he'd targeted; it completely disabled every single one of its systems, like an EMP, putting it straight into emergency mode.

Kai sank back in his chair. Exhausted. Spent.

He wasn't quite that invincible, apparently.

"Leader?" Evi called, concern evident in her intonation.

A psychic with a seriously good aim, she was one of the most valuable members of his group. She'd felt his faltering, no doubt. How he hated showing weakness.

"Shields are down. All fire on the platform," he ordered.

"Got it, over."

His fighters took care of the rest, firing on different parts of the command ship until it blew up. Hundreds of parts of Lordship hovered aimlessly in space, while others entered the atmosphere, and fell at high speed on the surface of Tenera. The cities were spared thanks to their shields – a few villages suffered. Kai had help dispatched to them almost immediately.

Now leaderless, the rest of the warlord's fleet fled back to their masters. They ran to their master, reporting impossibilities Enlil couldn't quite comprehend.

Kai only just managed to drag himself to his bed in the Zonian before collapsing. A light sleeper, generally alerted by the slightest sound, he passed out and stayed unconscious for hours, helpless.

Well, not quite. There was one wolf at his feet, four in front of his door, growling at anyone who dared get too close while their alpha was vulnerable.

When he awoke the next day, Kai left the Zonian to find most of his people assembled in the hangar, waiting front of the ship, understandably concerned.

"What now?" was the question on everyone's lips. And there was only one response, really.

For a blissful few weeks, he'd genuinely believed Hart's idea might have worked out, that they could simply claim this planet, or another world, as theirs, and live peacefully.

He would have another mission, a dangerous one. A raid at the heart of Vratis, to retrieve one of the warlord's most treasured possessions. The child. He owed her too much to leave her to her fate; beside, he'd made a promise, and he intended to keep it. But the future he'd envisioned had been peaceful, otherwise.

Now he saw it had simply been a fleeting dream.

"Now, we tend to our wounded and get ready. Tomorrow, we'll take the rest of this system. Then, the next world, and another one after that, until this sector is ours."

The only way they would have peace was war.

I t wasn't the first time they'd held a feast celebrating their victory, but this time, it was a grand thing. Never had they possessed this: the resources of an entire world. Still feeling weaker than he cared to admit, exhausted, Kai would have greatly preferred not to attend it, but his absence would have been noted.

The weather was kind, and no hall was grand enough to host their nation, so the feast was held in the streets.

The drums played a beat that reverberated through the entire city of Rumaul, intoxicating, thrilling. His people laughed, drank, fucked right there outside, barely bothering to hide in the shadows.

Kai rarely danced, but tonight he was almost

tempted. The enthralling beat resonated in his very heart. He felt the energy vibrate, calling to him in a strange way.

A few males and females came to attempt to coax him into joining them, but he remained seated in front of the main residence, deflecting their invitations as best he could.

"I wondered when it'd happen," said Krane, after observing him in silence for a good half hour.

"Finally saying whatever you have in mind?"

A good thing, too. The staring had been annoying.

"Aye. You depleted your energy. You need to recharge."

Kai tensed, neither denying nor confirming it.

"For most people, that would happen practically every day, after so much as using their mind to heat up a cup of tea," the know-it-all explained. "But the amount of power you have? Well, takes a lot to zap you."

It made an awful lot of sense, and, yet again, Kai wondered how Krane always had all the answers. It killed him, but he asked, "Recharge?"

The male standing to his left waved toward the crowd before them. "You see them do it. Now, and behind closed doors. Your power is molding energy as you see fit and releasing it into the world. Recharging it is harnessing it back in."

Kai frowned, not understanding Krane's meaning.

"Have you ever caused terror, pure terror, and enjoyed it?" asked the old male.

He remained silent. He caused terror every time he appeared in front of his enemy. And yes, a part of him enjoyed it, basked in it.

"Feelings are a powerful thing. They create an energy that stays right there, floating in the air. Unless it's harnessed, of course. Consciously or not, mages absorb it. Feed on it."

Now that the male put it into words, Kai knew what he meant. When his enemies trembled before him, it enthused him, increasing his reach through their mind, his power over them. He'd had no idea why, until now.

"'Course, you don't need to stick to horror and doom." Krane tilted his chin toward a female who had been attempting to catch Kai's eye for a while now. He'd thoroughly ignored her. "Fucking someone senseless does the trick, too. Pleasure is a feeling. A powerful one. The most powerful one, some might argue."

Kai snorted.

He hadn't touched a female in a long time. He didn't have the time for a casual partner. When his body desired release, he took matters in his own hand, always visualizing one face; that of the female he'd long ago seen himself standing next to. Stupid, but touching anyone else almost felt like a betrayal to a female he didn't yet know.

"Suit yourself." Krane shrugged. "But there's no one for you to torture right now, and you won't get better quickly without harnessing. Bet the headaches are a killer." They were, but Kai said nothing. Krane wasn't done talking. "Simple, ordinary feelings, they'll feed you over time. You'll be just fine in a week or so. *Or*, you could give a pretty thing one orgasm, and *boom*. Healed. Just like that."

More silence. Krane wasn't one to give up.

"Just saying, Kai. Today, you're just a little out of sorts, but there could come a time when you're completely depleted. When ninety-nine percent of your power is used up. You need to get used to this. It's part of what you are."

Kai finally spoke. "Stay out of my business."

The old male never would.

"You know, considering the way you scan faces

through the crowd, I guessed you're waiting for some-one. Anyone can see it."

The male always saw too much. Damn him.

"Whoever you're waiting for, she isn't here. She could be getting fucked herself right now, as we speak."

Kai was on his feet, facing Krane, looking at him in a way that would have made most tremble. The male smiled, glad he'd managed to get under Kai's skin. Dick.

"And I'd wager she wouldn't want you to suffer, or put yourself in danger by remaining weak."

Those words echoed through him, sounding true.

If the female was a mage, and she was feeling like this right now—heavy, nauseous, with a throbbing, lingering headache that wouldn't quit—he'd want it to stop. He'd want her to get better right then.

"You're turning into a good man, Kai. This won't change it. Sex is as casual as you make it. Tell her what you want from the very start, explicitly. Always pick a regular. A mage will take your energy, too—and that's intimate. Give her pleasures. You don't have to let her return the favor." Krane explained the rules Kai would live by for over a decade. Then, he cracked a smile. "And who knows? Maybe by the time you find that person you're looking for, you'll know your way around a clit. Might come in handy." He winked before walking back into the darkness of the residence.

Kai watched him leave, yet again wondering how the male appeared to know almost everything.

Krane could be mistaken, of course, but the old male had never said a thing that hadn't turned out to be true since the day they met.

He turned to the female who was still looking at him purposefully, playing with her hair. She was confident in her sexuality, and quite beautiful, too. Kai couldn't find it in himself to desire her. But for this experiment, she'd do.

He crossed the street, and, as he advanced, her teasing smile disappeared; she took a step back, as though suddenly questioning her resolve now that he was closer. Her back hit a marble column. Kai reached her and bent forward.

"Your name?" he asked.

"Bettra," she whispered, her bottom lip trembling.

Kai scanned her mind without being intrusive, just glancing at the surface through her eyes. "You're no mage."

She shook her pretty curls. "No, my sister's one of you. My whole family came two weeks ago."

Kai wondered if Krane had been able to tell somehow.

"You wanted my attention, Bettra. Now you have it."

She breathed in sharply, but despite the small spike of fear, Kai felt, and *smelled,* her arousal.

"I'm not going to want more than one night," he told her softly. "You understand?"

She nodded, her curls bouncing.

"Well then."

He had her curls bouncing again soon.

Kai hadn't been certain he'd actually take her. He hadn't wanted it, not really. Krane had prescribed an orgasm, and he'd planned on administering one before walking away, but after making the girl scream at the top of her voice with his fingers inside her, something primal, bestial, in him, took over. He fucked her for hours.

The old male had been right. The symptoms were gone, and he was back to his better self in no time. All that remained of his discomfort was a slight self-disgust in the morning. Kai wasn't simply back to normal; he'd never been stronger. Without any effort, he could feel every single Evris breathing in the building. He could feel his wolves, tell where they were.

He'd taken Bettra to the principal room in the residence he was occupying. Before fucking her in there, he'd intended to claim this room as his. Instead, he gave it to Hart, packed his things, and picked another suite, adding another rule to Krane's; he wasn't bringing females into his space ever again.

Kai did the one thing that helped calm him down: he took a knee, and breathed in and out, eyes closed. This should have looked like a submissive stance, but no mage would think so. They were so much more powerful when they cleared their minds, calmed down. When he knelt, those around him knew to be careful.

He wasn't preparing a large discharge of energy this time; just trying to think. When he got up again, he'd decided to accept this—his indifference mixed with his self-disgust. He accepted that he would do it again, next time his energy level went down. The encounter truly had made him more powerful. If fucking females he was indifferent to was part of him, he wouldn't deny himself. He had to survive. Nothing mattered more than living to see the day he'd glimpsed in his vision.

This was perhaps the first thing that molded him into a dark, coldhearted, ruthless monster.

The second step was losing wolves.

AFTER TENERA, the rest of the Krazu system fell to their rule within a year. Until then, they'd been quite informal about their quest, but as more planets were added to their territory, it became necessary to have a governing body set up. Authorities, enforcers, and people they answered to. They were a nation, and nations had leaders.

Kai wasn't much for politics. Talks and negotiations bored and frustrated him. He had no desire for power. Only peace. Building a world where their kind would be safe was his purpose, his goal in life. And finding that scarred woman one day, would be his reward. Nothing other than those two ends mattered to him.

Thus, he was quite stunned when the bulk of his people proposed to name him their ruler. Kai frowned, looking around the crowded hall, as though expecting a better option to materialize itself. But there was no one. Hart was the best second option, but Hart hadn't started this. Kai had. He wasn't the man their enemy feared and respected in equal parts. Kai was. Thousands of Evris looked to him, silently, expectantly.

"I'm no warlord," said Kai, his voice carrying through the vast hall. The words felt like lies. He pictured that image that never quite left his mind. For once, instead of looking at her, he focused on himself –

more specifically, his habit. A long white cloak with gold trim. Funny how he'd never stopped to *really* consider the implication. He'd be a warlord one day, if that vision came to pass.

"I wasn't born for this. Trained for this. Educated for this. I have no inclination for this."

At his side, Sky bumped her head on his leg, as though encouraging him to keep talking.

"But none of us were meant to have a place in this story. They would have us dead. For the last years, the last decades, every day we drew breath, we resisted their prejudice, their hatred, their tyranny. Surviving was our victory." Kai got up as the crowd nodded their agreement. "As I stand before you today, I'll tell you one thing. The world we'll build for our children will be better than this one. A kingdom where order and peace are law. Even if we need to forge it in fire."

The crowd cheered. Those words echoed through space and time, and, far from there, hearing every word clearly, Nalini bit her lips. So, that was it. Darkness was really coming. It meant Enlil's end, but at what price?

THE MEMBERS of Kai's fleet, mage or otherwise, were called "insurgents." People talked of them from one end of the sector to the next. Their numbers and their monopoly in a consequential system made them a force impossible to ignore. Soon, politicians and nobles started to openly support them. As they annexed more territories, their influence grew exponentially.

Kai took to wearing white; white and red. That way his people immediately recognized him, even at a distance. He heeded the little lady's advice and had a mask forged for when he appeared in public. A mask his enemies knew to fear. First came the messengers. Then the politicians. Kai Lor only appeared when the insurgents were done talking. He only appeared for destruction.

He left servants and children alive. Everyone else burned.

IMPERIAL YEAR 1219, when Nalini turned seventeen, Kai held three systems out of the nine in the Ratna Belt sector. The insurgents had become a growing concern, and Enlil decided to fight fire with fire. He went to the Wise and told them of mages in his sector. He demanded that he be allowed to train his own battalion of mages for his protection.

The Wise knew better than to deny his request. Exchanging glances, the four women and two men nodded in unison. "It is time," they agreed.

None of them had expected that the prophecy would

be easily thwarted. Killing those who developed aptitudes had only been a way to delay the inevitable,
until they couldn't hold off the danger any longer.

So, they started to plan.

TWELVE
COLDER

Kai grew cold. Colder every year. Colder yet when the first wolf of his pack died.

Strange. He courted death at every step —witnessed it, caused it sometimes. But Lok's demise took a piece of him.

The pack had grown. Sky had a litter of pups, so did Lok. But born around Evris who fed them and looked after them, rather than in the wild, frozen lands of Haimo where survival was a constant battle, the pups weren't quite the same animals. They weren't exactly tame, but somewhat closer to a dog than a wolf. The young pups bonded with some of his followers. Kai liked them well enough. Little Nura, for example. The pup who'd attached herself to Hart, his first advisor, had perfected an irresistible look that prompted her victims to spontaneously scratch her fur just where she wanted them to.

Lok fell in battle, taking a blow that would have killed him.

The insurgents and the warlord's forces rarely fought on the ground; most of their battles happened in space. When they got to the surface of a planet, it meant that the war was already won. No regular force could fight against mages. Knowing his wolves loved the exercise, Kai had never tried to prevent them from accompanying him. He'd grown complacent, too sure of himself. Used to blasters, he didn't see the metallic arrow coming at him during that fight. It might have pierced his energy shield; he'd never know. Lok jumped in the way.

As Kai stared at the fallen beast in disbelief, Sky howled high, sending the pack on a hunt. They ignored everything else in their path, everyone else, heading right to the archer.

The male who shot that arrow died screaming in agony, Kai saw to it. He got to him before the wolves were done ripping him apart, and dragged him away from the battle alive. Kai locked him in a cold, dark cell, and breached his mind, making him feel untold torments until his last breath. And then, he wished he could have made it last even longer.

Torturing that vile creature didn't help much. Nothing had ever prepared him for the pain and loss.

He carried Lok and headed to the one place that

seemed fit for her burial: Haimo, where she had a shrine fit for a king.

"We need to build them armor," was the first thing Kai said upon his return. "Exosuits."

He oversaw that project directly, needing a way to get his mind off the wolf's death. Finding ways to prevent the others from getting hurt worked as well as anything could have.

Kai learned quickly, reading every text he could access on biotech, familiarizing himself with the most advanced, responsive technology, until he knew as much as their best scientists. Wench, now a young man, who still trailed him whenever he could, had developed a knack for all kinds of tech during the time they spent in those labs. Above all, the kid was good with software and protocols. He'd make a fine hacker in time.

"Exosuits think for us; but honestly, it might freak an animal out. If something appeared out of nowhere to protect their heart, they might spook and end up putting themselves in danger," Elia, their best tech, explained.

"One way to find out."

Kai tried the suit on Sky. She wasn't impressed, at first; getting it to Her Furry Highness's high standards took a few tries. Finally, the wolves were safe.

Safer, in any case. The armor wasn't as responsive as Kai would have liked. He worried about it, but as the years passed, it proved effective.

Still, in 1216, he lost Nor to sickness. 1217 was the year Torj died of old age, peacefully. That left Nox and Sky, who seemed to hold on to the last pieces of his heart.

They were close to Torj's age.

Killing was easier each time he came back from burying a member of his pack.

What would he be like when Sky left this world?

Kai closed his eyes and searched inside himself, attempting to see a light, a piece of hope and goodness.

He cared about his people as a whole. Wanted them safe. Content, if possible. But that wasn't even close to what he felt for the beast at his side.

"You'll leave me one day soon" he told Sky.

Then he might truly be a monster.

He thought of the little girl who'd saved him twice, and of that female he still saw in his dreams. Perhaps they'd be enough to make him retain some degree of compassion, warmth.

Perhaps. Doubtful.

"Well, let's make sure that day doesn't come too soon, kid."

Only one male called him that.

"Krane."

The old male usually accompanied him for the beasts' funerals, but not this time; he'd stayed back. Kai was trying not to see it as a betrayal.

Ian Krane held a vial in his hand.

"This is a prototype concocted by them Imperials, and modified by the best in the market. Nanocytes built and developed to regenerate cells at an accelerated rate. One cell dies, it creates its replacement. This thing can regrow a damn arm overnight."

Kai had heard of this; everyone had. They whispered about it, grumbling about the way Imperials, high nobles, and the Wise selfishly kept it to themselves.

Immortality.

"You got your hands on a Rejuvenation Serum?" Kai sounded downright incredulous, for good reasons. This time, he had to ask, "All right, *who are you?*"

The old male winked and casually threw the vial his way.

"I'll do Nox. You do your beast. She'd rip my hand off. Press on the sides, a needle comes out. It'll work almost as soon as it's inside them. They'll just need a nap while the nanocytes sync."

Kai did as instructed, and Sky only bit him twice afterward. She growled at him for the rest of the day. Ian Krane managed well enough with Nox. Once they were done, they stared at each other defiantly.

Eventually, Kai just shook his head.

"You can get *immortality serums,* and you're giving it to animals."

The male made no sense.

"I'm giving it to the most important animals in this galaxy. These two die? How long before you kill us all in a tantrum, kid?"

Kai glared. "I don't throw tantrums."

He didn't. Did he?

"Yeah, sure. Whatever you say, boss."

Suddenly intrigued, Kai asked, "Did you take a shot?" Then, because the answer seemed obvious, he added, "How old are you?"

From what he knew of the advanced technology, the nanocytes worked to replace cells the moment they died, which meant that those who took it didn't age, or die of most natural causes. Although Kai liked to call him old, Krane had the appearance of a healthy man of forty, perhaps; but if he was immortal, it meant nothing. He could be hundreds of years of age. More, perhaps. The first of those shots had been developed roughly thirteen hundred years ago.

Krane laughed and walked away, calling out, "You're wanted in Control. PunyLord sent envoys to negotiate a treaty. The Coats are divided."

Kai sighed. The Coats, as Krane liked to call the senators who were their voice in the High Council of Ratna, formed of envoys from each planet, were *always* divided.

The treaty was everything he'd ever desired. It offered peace. Enlil swore to leave him alone as long as they stuck to their systems and never moved to conquer more of his territories. It also offered something else, something Kai never desired and wouldn't have sought. The warlord had done his research and found out where Kai had come from. By edict of Enlil, Kai would be made a Hora, Lord of Haimo.

The very thought disgusted him, but he had to think of the bigger picture.

"This treaty means safety," he said, causing some of his senators to nod enthusiastically. Half of the Coats started to speak. He lifted one hand, and they fell silent. "But," Kai added, "Enlil will never keep his word. He needs time to regroup. He'll attack when it suits him."

Kai was turning in quite the Coat, agreeing with everyone.

"So, what now?" Hart prompted.

Kai closed his eyes, searching for the answer. Then, he lifted his hand, and a pen floated to him. He stabbed the quill into his thumb, drawing blood, and signed.

"Now," he replied, "we take this time, get ready, and wait for the snake to launch. History will recall us as those who accepted peace, and him as the one who broke it."

The strategy was foolish of Enlil. They were many now, but in months, years? Then children they fiercely protected within the walls of their base would be ready to fight. Time was their ally, turning their army into an unrelenting force.

Enlil attacked in 1222. In 1226, Kai's armies flew right at the heart of Vratis.

THIRTEEN
DARKNESS

A thousand years before this war, their race had inhabited Tejen, one single planet, living there quite peacefully and in harmony with all living things. There were great beasts that breathed fire, and Evris were their companions. When they came of age, the warriors amongst them went to the heart of the forest and sought one out, binding their hearts together.

This sacred bond with nature, cultivated with love, strengthened them. Some lines of Evris, known for their valor, were blessed with a link with nature. Magic, they'd call it.

Mages were revered and celebrated. All of them tamed dragons with ease, brought rain when the fields were dry, and stopped tornadoes from destroying cities. Mages were their protectors. Even more so when aliens came down from the skies.

The invading creatures had sought their world's resources. Evris fought, but, against the technology of a race that could travel through the infinity of space, their weapons were little more than sticks and stones. Every one of their weapons—except magic.

She was born during that war. A child. No one knew whose. What they knew was that one day, she stopped time. Another day, she called night, moving the sun by her strength of will. That's when they started to call her Darkness. The child grew in power every year. Finally, she destroyed a thousand enemy ships in one blast.

Once the enemies were gone, one thing remained. Darkness. A child who could kill them all effortlessly. Who wanted to take that risk?

The Wise council of mages at the head of her order voted, and they voted wrong. Only one voice spoke against their decision that day.

The vote was a sentence: death. For the safety of all, the child was condemned.

If they'd managed to kill her then, the consequences might have been less destructive. They didn't. How could they?

Darkness ran alone. She didn't stay so for long. Worshipped by some, admired by others, she soon had followers. The Darklings. They took over the world and cornered the Wise, who fled, along with their supporters, using the foreign alien technology to leave their original world behind.

Darkness followed, determined to destroy her enemies. The first inhabitable sector she found was what was now called the Ratna Belt. There, she was eventually defeated, but a seer foresaw her return.

The Wise settled on Magneo, forming their new order there. The Empire. They enthroned a leader without magic and ordered that every child born with power be put to rest for the good of the entire universe.

Darkness came back. Again and again and again. And each time, before it came of age, before it became conscious of the extent of its power, it was killed.

Until now.

For the thousandth time, Nalini closed her eyes and tried as hard as she could to see more. Most of the books about these ancient times were nothing short of fairy tales. Those that seemed even remotely accurate had been written by the Wise, who may or may not be biased on that subject. But it was ever so important that she grasped what had happened the first time, in order to avoid the same end.

But past and future were clouded. No, not clouded.

Purposefully blocked. As though a force consciously prevented her from seeing more. That made little sense to Nalini. This only occurred when she attempted to see her own future in details.

She cursed and got up, feeling helpless, frustrated, and confused.

OVER THE DECADES, centuries, the Imperials grew in size and power, discovering and conquering more worlds. Yet they always left the Belt relatively alone, allowing it to be ruled by its leader, rather than considering it as a territory of the Imperials. It was still mostly inhabited by the descendants of those who'd accompanied Darkness and settled there. Over time, Evris had succeeded in weaning most of the magical blood from their families, but still, in that sector, there had always been more children developing those aptitudes, as most of them had Darkling blood.

Vratis had been the City of Darkness. Still, it showed. Even a thousand years later, there were spells guarding against enemies, pushing Kai back every time he attempted an offensive.

Kai had no clue how to fight against these powers. A magnetic field, he would have been prepared for, but this was something else. The entire planet was coated in pure magic. An elemental magic he recognized—fire and something more. It felt like his.

Instead of attacking the main system, he took the surrounding planets, cutting the warlord off, leaving him nothing but his one planet.

Vratis was used to receiving provisions from all over the sector; the planet was a center of commerce and politics, with leisure palaces and luxury retreats. The siege didn't last long. In 1226, at age 33, Kai entered the warlord's palace as its new ruler. Enlil's son had killed his own father in his sleep and called to surrender.

Now, Kai was done. He didn't hold every single planet in the Belt, but he didn't need to. No one would contest his absolute rule. His laws would stand. They'd have peace.

He should have felt fulfilled. Happy, even. Not lost, confused, and disappointed.

He shouldn't be. He hadn't expected the female to miraculously appear the moment he'd reached his goal. Still, something felt wrong.

The only person who might have an answer—as he had an answer for all things, or so it seemed—had left the previous day.

"Listen, kid, I gotta dash. There's somewhere I need to be."

"Sure," he'd replied, shrugging indifferently. "When will you be back?"

"I won't come back."

Kai had stared at Ian Krane in complete disbelief. Imagining a world where the old male wasn't by his side barely made sense.

But it had happened the moment they'd landed on Vratis. Krane was gone, taking Nox with him.

Strange how hard it was to see what one has, until it's taken.

Kai was purposefully not thinking of his old friend, mentor—whatever Krane had been—and his unexpected defection. There was too much to do, too much to plan.

At least, Wench had good news about the girl. He could hold on to that.

Kai followed his young mechanic to the surveillance level, where the boy prepped him by saying, "Okay, so we found her and compiled one single file for you. It took a while; there were years of data. We've fast-forwarded through the irrelevant stuff; so overall, you have about three hours of recordings. I could just tell you what happened, but...."

"No," he replied, adamant. "I'll watch it."

Wench smiled goofily, visibly proud as he handed his

lord a slim database controller. Catching himself in time, for once, Kai told him, "Well done."

He glanced down and saw three letters marked in an ancient phonetic alphabet on top of the database. NA-LI-NI.

He recognized that name. Down to his bones.

FOURTEEN
RUTHLESS

Kai remained motionless and entirely focused, his eyes taking in every single second of the child's life. He curled his fists at the start and never relaxed them.

His companions had taken cautious steps back as he grew dimmer, fiercer, each time the warlord's enforcers came to shave her head and force her on machines. They pricked her with needles constantly, taking some of her blood to analyze it. They forced her to wear brain scanning devices and made her use her powers until she screamed out in pain. They locked her in cages and shocked her with energy, as a punishment for any degree of failure and, sometimes, for no reason at all. Weekly. Her energy was stored in vials; for what purpose, Kai didn't know.

Year after year, this was her normal.

The child was called Nalini. Her folder said so. Nalini never flinched, never complained, never asked for anything. Fast-forwarding through it, Kai felt like screaming. Her meeting with him was only one of the million trials life had thrown at her. And it wasn't the only time she fought, either.

Twelve. Out of the fifteen mages she was asked to scan in her lifetime, she'd freed twelve of them.

Sometimes, in the darkness, she gathered her knees to her chest and held them close. Kai had believed he knew what rage was, but he'd had no clue, not until he saw this. He needed to destroy something, just as soon as he was done watching these horrific recordings.

Years passed, and nothing changed for her. She grew up into a pretty young thing. The warlord noticed. Kai half expected him to try to touch her, given the way he looked at her. If he had, by all gods, he would have found a way to bring him back to life in order to torture him for the rest of eternity. But Enlil had other ideas.

It was Imperial year 1219, a few years after Kai had openly started to take over Enlil's territories at the fringes. He called Nalini to his throne room, in the presence of his seven advisors.

"Here's my favorite mage," he called fondly.

She pretended to smile.

The warlord got down from his seat and gestured Nalini to follow him, as he went to the very balcony where Kai had stood a few hours ago.

She trailed him as he spoke; drones followed them, so Kai didn't miss a second of the exchange. A small delegation was waiting for them on the balcony—two guards and a noble dressed in white and gold, like Enlil.

"Our men have fought against this barbarian, this Kai Lor, for years now, and yet, he still escapes us."

The direct criticism didn't faze the girl. "Kai Lor is beyond my reach, my lord," she lied. Kai knew she lied. She'd appeared out of nowhere when he'd needed help years ago; no doubt she could easily have located him, had she wished to. "I can't see anything from him."

"Yes, yes, I know you tried. It's quite all right to admit that there are creatures more powerful than you."

The teenager attempted no reply.

"Given our predicament, the Wise have authorized that we recruit more mages to our cause."

She didn't so much as blink.

"We've selected a handful of potential recruits. A dozen children. You'll train them, bring them up to speed."

A nod.

"I'm so very proud of you, Nali," the warlord gushed. "And to let it be known that I reward loyalty, I will now welcome you into my family."

Kai felt sick to his stomach. Enlil gestured to the male in white and gold, a tall, pale Evris, in his early thirties perhaps. "You'll wed my son, child."

Nalini inclined her head compliantly. "If you so wish."

The warlord laughed. "Not even a smile. But surely you'll be glad to reclaim your title now."

She lifted a brow.

"You were born a Nova, princess of Itri."

For the first time, one emotion was evident in her expression, a faint distaste.

"That name means little to me," she said.

Enlil inclined his head like he understood. "I suppose it wouldn't. How long has it been since you've heard from your family now?"

She remained silent.

"You'll be given more freedom. Quarters of your own. And should your children possess a fraction of your strength, we'll be very blessed indeed."

No doubt that's why the greedy male had chosen her

as his son's incubator. How old was she, anyway? He glanced down to the date displayed on the monitor, and did the math; she'd said she was twelve back in 1214, so that made her seventeen in 1219. A child still. Kai was moments from erupting.

"There's just one little thing," the warlord said, a cruel smile on his lips. "A small matter. Consider it a formality, really."

He lifted his hands, and the two guards standing behind his son parted, revealing a young boy bound in energy chains. Nalini didn't react to his presence. Like she'd expected it.

"You've never shown anything but unwavering compliance, child. But to give you a place amongst my family, I need to know you're committed to our cause." He pointed to the child. "This mageling is belligerent and refuses to comply at every turn."

Kai froze, expecting the cold order before it crossed Enlil's lips. "Kill it."

Nalini nodded, lifting her hand. One of the guards' weapons lifted from its holster and floated to her. An energy whip. The cruelest one she could have picked. Kai had seen the sort of damage it inflicted on a person. She was going to have to hit a few times to kill.

He half wished he was weaker and could have looked away from the holographic recording. But he watched her, never blinking, ready to let her destroy the dream, destroy the illusion. His hopes for their entire race had rested upon the actions of that child. By killing a five-year-old to save her own skin, she was going to destroy it. Kai understood it, and he knew he had to watch her do it, if only so he could move on.

The girl took one step and smiled. "It's okay," she said, and Enlil beamed with glee.

Only, Kai realized, she wasn't talking to him at all. Her eyes were fixed on the child. The boy stopped trembling. He nodded almost imperceptibly, cluing Kai in a second before it started.

He stared speechless, barely believing his eyes.

Obeying an order no one could hear, the child ducked to the floor. Nalini's flaming whip cracked the air, hitting both guards so hard they dropped to the floor; she leaped and grabbed the child, throwing him on her shoulder before raising her hand to protect them both. Enlil and his son had both started shooting at them with blasters. The blasts hit an energy wall.

"You're going to regret this, girl," the warlord swore.

Nalini shrugged. "Doubtful. Your son isn't my type. Too pasty. And, boy, ever heard of working out?"

Enlil seemed shocked, with good reason. This was the first time he ever saw that smile. That spunk. The fire she'd hidden since the moment she entered his palace.

"Well, so long everybody," she said, before jumping down over the balcony railing.

Kai's stomach dropped. The drop might have killed her.

Her red whip flashed, hooking on a large, heavy statue, and the fugitives safely dangled down from it until they'd reached the ground.

"Guards! Follow her! Set every fucking drone in the palace on the seer!"

Kai was grateful for the order; he *needed* to know what had happened next. It took minutes for the first drones to find her in the palace's gardens. He remembered these very sculptures, fountains, and bushes. Eight years before her, Kai had followed the path out toward the entrance of the warlord's palace. Nalini was running in a different direction now. Deeper into the gardens. It made no sense. In that direction, there was nothing but cliffs. Endless cliffs dropping into a torrential hell.

Hundreds of guards followed on foot and in speeders and light fighters, all shooting in her direction in vain. She arrived at the cliffs and talked to the child on her back, ever so softly. Kai couldn't hear a word, but he could guess they were reassuring, infusing strength into him.

Both of Nalini's eyes had turned a pure blue. The boy held on tighter to her back, burying his little head between her shoulder blades. She praised him before sitting on the ground, legs crossed, eyes closed, like there weren't hundreds of enemies closing in on her. Kai understood; he knelt when he needed to clear his mind and push his own powers. Her enemy stilled, confused, wondering if she was surrendering, but there was no doubt that if they'd tried to close in around her, they would have hit an invisible energy wall.

When her eyes opened again, they were both gold this time. Blue for peace and gold when she attacked, Kai realized. Most of the time, they were both shades because she was always on her guard.

Nalini popped up and started running at full speed toward the cliff. Guards shouted, attempting to catch her before she committed suicide; their orders had been to bring her back alive, no doubt. Kai fucking hoped they'd managed to stop her from jumping to her death.

A high-pitched cry broke through the skies; the surveillance drones, guards, and everyone else zeroed in on the direction where it had come from, confused at first, and then downright incredulous.

An entire flock of humongous firebirds flew their way at full speed. The wild, untamable animals hated people; sightings were rare and never during the day. Yet there were at least two dozen of them.

"Cover!" a commander screamed, and the enforcers ducked.

Firebirds were dangerous, not unlike the dragons of legend, and these clearly intended them harm; focused on them with talons outstretched, screaming as they dove down on the enforcer battalions. Blasters could do little against their impenetrable iron feathers, and the enforcers' exouniforms wouldn't stop their fire.

But the flock had little interest in the enforcers at all.

Nalini jumped while they were distracted. The largest bird's talons hooked around her left arm, digging into her flesh as he pulled her up and flew her through the Vratis torrents.

The guards watched, helpless. Drones flew along, following her at a distance, as no machine could rival a goddamn firebird in speed.

Kai's eyes narrowed, as facts started to compute in his mind.

"Zero in the drone closest to her," he ordered.

He started pacing, his reality taking on a brand-new meaning. A confusing, yet utterly logical turn.

"This is as close as we can get without getting blurry," Wench said.

It was close enough. Close enough to clearly see what he needed to see. Once they reached the shore, the bird's talon unhooked from her arm. The bird hadn't meant any harm, but it certainly wasn't used to chartering people around; his sharp claws bit at the girl's flesh, leaving a clear, bloody mark up her arm to her shoulder and then extending a little on her throat. A wound that would leave a scar.

A scar he knew. She'd proudly get tattoos around it, no doubt celebrating the day she'd grasped her freedom.

Nalini talked to the child, who jumped down her back and looked away reluctantly. She plunged her fingers inside her deep, ugly wound. Thick, dark blue blood coated her hand. She winced but kept her mouth shut. Finally, she pulled out something—her tracker, Kai realized. Then she turned, one hand lifted toward the drones, and the image shut down as the machines exploded.

HE DIDN'T NEED any more proof at this point, but Kai moved to the command panel and pulled up the last clear image they'd recorded.

Photo manipulation wasn't his strongest suit; again,

he had to rely on Wench. "Age her," he directed. "Add hair."

The male pulled up the right program.

"What sort of hair?" he asked.

"Dark, with strands of red."

He could also have told him about the tattoos and the face jewelry. He didn't need to. Once Wench was done, the program showed exactly what he'd expected to see.

It was her. The child. The female he'd seen in his vision. They were one and the same. Nalini Nova.

He'd never felt so stupid in his entire life.

S *even years ago.*

SHE NEEDED to stop the bleeding, keep herself and the crying child calm—-but more importantly, she needed transport off this planet, out of this system. *Now.* Because Enlil would soon have the entire place on lockdown and destroyers blasting everything unauthorized trying to take off from Vratis.

"You're okay. We're okay," she told the boy. "Listen, if we don't get out of here now, we're going to get in big, big trouble. You think you can run with me?"

He nodded while pouting.

Good. She couldn't carry him long while bleeding out like this.

Nalini looked in every direction before closing her eyes. Eyes were deceiving. When they opened again, flashing amber, she knew where to go. "Let's get moving."

She found a small, wealthy village and stopped at the first home. An elegant young couple was having dinner. They looked at her, distraught and terrified. Nalini didn't know either of them. They were probably good people. They didn't deserve to have their free will stripped away. No one did.

Right now, it didn't matter.

Her eyes gold, she stared them down.

The female moved first, heading to the bathroom to get the medic pack out. The male started to describe his transport, telling her exactly how to unlock the security system around it.

"You need to get out of here," she told them, another order. Although they'd not done any of it of their own will, they'd be punished, tortured, and probably killed for helping her if they were found. "Now."

They obeyed this compulsion just like the others. Nalini didn't let the guilt eat at her conscience over the violation. Then, and later, she did what she had to.

And she lived.

NOW.

NALINI WOKE up to a familiar feeling; only, it was a thousand time stronger. Kai, she knew. But it didn't feel like there was anything wrong with him that day.

She remained in her bed, breathing in and out, willing herself to clear her mind. She'd had the dream again. That dream. The jumbled mixture of visions that made her both want to seek out and run from Kai. It exhausted her and left her restless.

"Nali!" a little voice called out, pulling her back to reality. "Client."

She lifted her head toward the small window in her room. It was barely dawn. They'd better pay extra.

She stretched and dragged a tunic up her tired limbs before emerging. "Have you been up all night again?" she asked the boy.

Kronos was a night owl. At thirteen, the boy was allowed to keep whatever sleeping habits he wanted, as long as he was up on time for school and did his chores. Nalini was pretty certain many a parent would have disagreed, but well, she wasn't much of a parent at all.

After running from Vratis together seven years ago, they'd stuck together, traveling as brother and sister. No one questioned the story; Kronos was dark of hair, and while they didn't share many features, they certainly did have a similar snarky attitude.

It had taken a while to find somewhere she felt safe. At first, they'd moved often, always looking over their shoulder. But strangely, she'd finally settled on Itri, her home world.

Enlil had every guard looking for her in every single system of the Ratna Belt. There was a humongous price on her head, and it had recently changed to a higher amount. However, thankfully, her poster showed a little monk in white, with her signature heterochromatic eyes. She could genuinely look an enforcer right in the eye without them so much as lifting a brow now.

Nali's eyes were both blue these days. She'd learned to control it, as long as she kept her powers in check when she had company, they stayed that way. She'd started growing her hair out right away. After over half a dozen years, it reached her lower back. She often had it colored for fun. Right now, the bottom part of it was bright red. She never wore white, cream, or other boring shades she'd had to stick to in her youth. In fact, most of her wardrobe was black.

The one thing she couldn't change was her DNA, and the authorities *did* have that in their records. So she did her very best to stay away from officials. As it turned out, she wasn't the only drifter who preferred to stay away from authority's radar. A lot of them had ended up in the Var.

The system had recently acquired a reputation for being quite loose with protocols. They rarely did a proper census, and no one was required to identify themselves for simple things like buying milk. Nalini had heard whispered theories. People said the royals of Itri had a thing against the warlord because of what had happened to their poor little daughter. She smiled, liking the sentimentality behind that theory. From what she knew of her parents, it was unlikely, though. They probably simply preferred to keep things vague to lower their taxes.

Nalini opened her door, finding a middle-aged female in front of it. She sighed.

"Again?"

Sofra Blue's son had needed her help four times in as many months. He managed to get into a fight every other weekend, and he rarely won any of them.

But Sofra was a baker, and she paid in breads and cakes. Nalini wasn't about to complain. She unhooked her bag from the back of her door, and followed the female through the streets of Fruja, which were always peaceful in the early morning. It would be a warm day, she could tell. There was barely any wind coming from the Endless Sea, and although the sun had just risen, the air already felt heavy. Nalini didn't mind winter, but summer really was exhausting.

Beau Blue needed stitches and an ointment that day. On her way back, she was called to the Craden household; Marja's pregnancy made her drowsy. Nalini prepared an herbal drink and came home with eggs for her trouble.

She'd picked a simple town. People had little money and little use for it; everything was bartered.

She'd fallen face first into healing. Her schooling hadn't prepared her for many practical professions, but she'd developed an interest in botany as a child. Enlil had seen no harm in letting her spend some time in his inner garden, as a reward for good behavior. He'd made relevant books available on the subject. Therefore, she knew which plants eased fever, which ones calmed upset stomach or slowed down an infection. She also knew how to grow them.

Someone saw her prepare an infusion for Kronos when he'd caught a bug years ago; she'd asked if Nalini could do the same for her own child, in exchange for a payment in barter. The rest was history.

Nalini smiled each time she imagined Enlil's scowl,

had he known that one of his rare kindnesses towards her had given her a profession.

Once home, she tended to her plants, which needed a little more love than usual in the heat, before sitting down for breakfast, at last.

It was then that the feeling came back. *Kai.*

He'd always been there, every day of her life since they'd first met. But today, something really was different. It was as though he was calling to her, whispering her name. She should have—could have—ignored it. But she gave in. Searched through the link, their bond, and tugged on it. The next instant, her consciousness was sucked into a void, so fast she had to close her eyes, and then violently pushed back out.

Her surroundings had vanished, replaced by his.

He stood in his room—she knew it was his room. Large, plain, and extremely tidy. God, the male seriously needed someone to mess his life up a little. She bet his underpants were folded. Maybe even ironed.

Kai was looking out the window. Nalini glanced in the direction of his gaze and gasped out loud. She knew this place. Vratis. He'd made it to Vratis.

She'd heard about his civil war, everyone had. As systems fell to mages, nobles had started to panic around Itri, like their kind had everywhere else; in her village, it was nothing more than campfire stories people discussed indifferently. The rulers of the world had little interest in places like Fruja.

In any case, Nalini had expected to hear that he'd taken over from Enlil someday. She'd seen it quite clearly. She just hadn't expected it quite so soon.

As she gasped, Kai turned sharply, hand lifted defensively, fire in his grasp. His expression changed when he took her in. She saw shock and something else, too.

He dropped his hand.

"Nalini."

It was the first time he'd said her name; she should have wondered how he knew it at all.

"Akai." She looked around. "You made it, then." His eyes trailed her as she awkwardly kept on watching everything but him. "Congratulations are in order."

"Where are you?" he asked.

She frowned. "At home."

"Where?" he repeated insistently, his voice made darker as he used his power to emphasize his command.

Like that would work on her.

She dropped her eyes. There was a reason she hadn't sought him out seven years ago, although she'd been dying to. She knew he would have helped her. Taken care of her. Cold and intense as he was, his unrelenting, intense gaze caught on hers like he was trying to set her soul on fire, he would have helped, if only because he owed her.

But she was a powerful seer, and that power couldn't fall into the hands of a male like him. A male who was just another—a younger, more appealing—Enlil.

"I'll find you."

She'd heard a warlord say that to her before. The first time, it had been a threat, barked in rage, promising torture and vengeance.

Kai almost whispered it, softly. Yet, this time, she shivered.

She should have been frightened. He was stronger than she was now. If he recalled his fire and set it against her, she'd be reduced to ashes. She should be careful of him. Take a step back, perhaps. Kai was also infinitely tall, with large shoulders and the presence of a male of war. Physically, he dominated her.

Yet fear had nothing to do with the reason why she shivered.

Nalini hadn't seen him in twelve years. Now they were both adults. Now, she knew enough of the world, and she recognized the longing and need burning her insides as she watched him. Something pulled her toward him in a way she hadn't expected to ever feel. Not after twenty-four years of utter indifference toward the other sex.

"Why?" she asked him.

His answer was simple and immediate. "Because you belong here."

Here, in Vratis, in her cold room, where she'd be locked away until he needed her council.

She forced herself to take one step back, then another one, and, on the other side of the sector, she blinked, back in her body.

Enlil had told her he'd had other seers over the years, and the others had all made mistakes at some point. When Nalini predicted a course of action, it was accurate. Always.

Kai wanted to use the strongest seer in the universe, like the warlord who'd come before him. Of course he did. With her, he'd be unstoppable.

She might have given in to temptation, all the while knowing that the only male who'd ever made her feel this way wanted her for her power. But her dreams and nightmares served her well. In half of those visions, their worlds still burned at his hand. As long as that future was a possibility, she'd stay away. She had to.

KAI REMAINED immobile for all of three seconds as Nalini disappeared before his eyes. Then, he gave up on attempting to keep it in. The instant he let go of the careful hold he'd had on his power, everything in his room exploded, turned to ashes and dust. The windows were shattered; the walls cracked.

He regained control after a beat. It wouldn't do to destroy his new home in a fit of rage.

A battalion of soldiers rushed in, ready to take orders, no doubt believing someone had bombed him.

"My lord, is everything—"

"Get my ship ready," he ordered. "We're pushing through to Pender today."

There were thirty planets divided in nine systems in the Ratna Belt. Seventeen of those planets were under his control now.

Nalini was somewhere on one of the thirteen planets left. She wouldn't have left the sector, of that he was sure. The Imperial territories were far too dangerous for an Evris who possessed magic. But she'd also stay away from the worlds under his thumb, knowing other mages would recognize her for what she was.

He'd take them all.

Every planet, every city, every single village, until he'd found her.

Kai took Pender within the next seven months. As it was the main planet in the Darien system, the entire system fell to his rule in no time. Itri was his next target, but he surprised everyone involved by preferring diplomacy this one time.

He spoke to the Novas in a private council; none of his men knew what was said, but, next thing they knew, Itri was theirs, too. The Novas retained their titles and their resources. As the system had already outlawed slavery, their main concession was guaranteeing safety to those born with magic. And, of course, some of Kai's troops stayed behind to see to the transition.

Nalini was genuinely surprised to see soldiers in exosuits parading around Fruja. They really were thorough, if they visited their irrelevant little village.

She pulled her hood around her face and resolved to stay home while they were in town.

"They're pretty cool," Kronos told her. "They have weapons, but I saw one of them make something float in his hand. Right out there, in public."

The child's eyes were widened in wonder. The very notion of not having to hide magic was as foreign as it was wonderful. Nalini smiled, hoping that the world would become a place where they were safe to do just that someday. But it wasn't. Not yet. Not for her, in any case.

"What do you think they're doing here?" the boy wondered.

She shrugged. "There's a lot of disagreement over Kai Lor Hora's rule, from the talk. Maybe they're looking for insurgents."

Or for her.

Probably both.

Kronos snorted. "Here? Yeah, right. Like something half that interesting would ever happen *here*."

He hated their little village. To be honest, so did Nali. There was a whole world out there they could fly to, explore.

But the village was safe, for the thirteen-year-old boy and for her.

Or so she thought, until half a dozen men stormed into her house.

THEY'D WATCHED her carefully avoid them and avert her eyes, and, for their simplistic commander, that was enough to warrant a forceful questioning. What reason would a pretty young female have to be quite so wary of them if she didn't have anything to hide?

Eager to prove himself, Yurik Grans ordered the raid that sealed his fate.

As a seer, Nalini was always a little frustrated when something she hadn't seen at any point occurred, but her own future, and things in the immediate future, were often clouded. She knew the date when the sun of their system was going to die in millions of years. She knew that the palace where her parents lived was going to burn in less than a decade. She saw it clearly, marked in stone. However, she'd be hard pressed to predict what time she was going to wake up the next morning.

Nalini froze, eyes wide open, as her door was kicked open.

Her surprise didn't last long. The next second, the hilt of her whip floated to her extended hand. The instant the object touched her palm, the whip flashed red, her power coursing through it, coating it in something far deadlier than the energy it had been built to contain.

"Trust me when I say you don't want to do this, boys," she roared darkly.

Nalini wasn't one for violence, given a choice. She detested war, and there were always alternatives to fighting, as far as she was concerned. But these men had entered *her* home armed and without an invitation. So, yes, responding with a whip in hand seemed appropriate.

"You're mage."

Yurik was confused for an instant. It didn't compute. He'd imagined that she had some loyalist intel, but loyalists, the old warlord's supporters still fighting against Kai in every system, were firmly anti-magic. He might have made a mistake here.

He took a step forward, hand up. "Look—"

The female cracked her whip. "Come closer, I dare you."

He was no coward. Lord Kai himself had remarked upon his courage in the past. But that female made him freeze and want to turn back.

He was about to explain he'd just assumed she was an insurgent, and maybe even apologize, when something hit him from the side. Something fast and powerful. Yurik's finger automatically pulled the trigger of his blaster, aiming and shooting at the threat.

The threat stopped and fell. A long silent second passed as what he'd done sank in.

It was a boy. Just a little boy, not even a teenager. And he'd shot him right between the eyes.

HE FELT it from worlds away. Heard the scream like she was right next to him. The hole forming in her bright, soft, loving heart hurt his, practically bringing him to his knees. He couldn't breathe.

Nalini was hurting like she'd never hurt before. And for the first time, he was the one who instinctively travelled to her.

He took in the scene before his eyes.

Nalini was on the floor, crying over the body of a child. The boy she'd saved from Enlil. Kai recognized him from the recordings he'd watched, although he was much older now. And dead.

Yurik stood speechless and trembling at his own action. "Lord—"

He didn't let him finish that sentiment. Kai lifted his hand, and the commander fell, screaming in pain.

He took in her simple, large, one-room dwelling in

one glance. It was disorderly; she hadn't made her small bed, on one side, or the smaller one tucked away next to it. Dark clothing hung behind a chair. His eyes settled on her bedding. It smelled like her, no doubt. He hooked his hands together, behind his back, to fight against his compulsion to make things just right.

Kai advanced toward Nalini carefully, slowly. He crouched close to her and put his hand on her back.

"You did this."

Her spiteful accusation didn't faze him. He hadn't, and yet he had. Everything his enforcers did was a reflection of his rule. Instinctively, Kai just ran his palm up and down her back in a comforting motion that soothed them both. He'd never done that to a living soul, not even Sky.

Finally, he dared to look directly at the boy. Nalini loved him, that much was clear. He was her child, in a way. In another world, Kai might have cared for him, too.

Kai put his free hand on the boy's forehead, covering the wound he didn't want to see, and moved it down to close his eyes.

As his hand caressed the still-warm skin of the dead boy, Kai felt something. Something pulling at him, tugging at the edge of his mind.

Frowning, he gave into his instinct and pushed energy through his mind. Nalini turned her glare on him, a protest ready on her lips, no doubt. Kai saw her open her mouth from the corner of his eye. Whatever colorful words she'd planned to say, they never crossed her lips. A faint light lit up inside Kai's palm, and transferred to the boy's body.

He felt it being absorbed, taken in by the lifeless child.

After a few instants, they felt it; the child's presence was back. He wasn't breathing, not yet. But there was a spark of life inside this body; as mage, they could decipherer the presence of a life form.

"That's not possible," Nalini breathed next to him. "He is dead."

Kai shut her out and kept on pushing everything he had, everything he was. Back on Vratis, his nose bled blue and his body shook.

"Fuck." Nalini rushed to place her own hand on top of his. Without hesitation, she trusted him and relinquished all of her strength to him.

He'd never felt power like this before. The instant he let her in, he truly, physically, felt connected to every part of the universe. Each flower, animal, each dying star, each crying mother birthing daughters and sons, and each old couple dying hand in hand were part of him. He saw them all, past and future forever interlinked. And he felt her love for it all. The pureness of her beautiful soul.

Kai had the power to make the earth beneath him shake, reduce worlds to cinder, and Nalini was light to his dark. Life to his destruction.

But right now, they were together, finishing the circle that should never have been broken. His body stopped struggling in his cold, dark chamber. Right then, everything was effortless. Golden energy coated their intertwined fingers. Life and death, that they could mold like gods. The strands of translucent matter entered the child's broken body and lit it up before fading.

The boy's chest rose and fell. And again. Kai moved his hand, still coated in blood. There wasn't so much as a scratch or a scar where the child had been shot.

"Kronos," she whispered through her tears.

The boy blinked. "Wow. Talk about trippy."

She laughed, cried, and pulled him to her arms, holding him close.

Then, Nalini's glare lifted to him. Cold. Unforgiving.

"I'm sorry."

No response crossed her lips.

"We don't shoot children, Nalini. This was visibly an accident. The party responsible has already paid for it." He waved toward the dead male in her foyer.

"Get out."

Everything in him rebelled against it, but right then, he had no hopes of getting through to her, he knew it. With time, she'd forgive him. She'd be grateful for his help, too. But now all she knew was that her child had died because of his troops.

He tilted his head, and his stunned enforcers rushed out the door.

How he wished Nalini would just come home, where she'd be safe. Today, it had been his side. Next time, it could be insurgents or Imperials. She could take care of herself, but he didn't want her to have to.

"Thank you, mister," the boy called out as he disappeared, returning to his body.

He found it in himself to smile. "Take care of her."

The moment he regained consciousness, reentering his body crouched on the floor and immobile, he went to his command board and checked on Yurik Grans's placement.

The Val. A little village in the outback of the most irrelevant county of Itri, the principal planet in the system. He pulled up his map and marked it with a red pin. If he was right, Nalini and the boy would be gone by morning. He recorded the intel, nonetheless.

He'd purposefully look for similar locations in the future. Remote, yet close enough to a consequential system for her to have access to every type of technology and recent news. The sort of place those who were running from something preferred.

And she *was* running. From him.

Kai could have had her trailed, but that seemed counterproductive now. She wouldn't be receptive to anything he had to offer today.

He had to do better. Be better. Represent something she'd approve of. He'd do his very best, and then soon, she'd be by his side.

That, he refused to doubt for one instant.

"**W**hy do we have to go?"

Nalini groaned. "I thought you hated Fruja."

"Sure, I hate Fruja. But running in the middle of the night without even packing my stuff isn't what I had in mind."

"Then pack! You have two minutes."

Nothing she owned held any sentimental value to her. Before getting to Itri, she'd managed to sell her healing skills to some people willing to pay a fair amount for a decent healer who didn't ask questions. She'd used most of what she'd made to buy her ship, but she still had a little money hidden here and there. She picked it up from under their chest of drawers, behind their sofas, and under their mattresses as Kronos kept on fussing over his meager possessions.

"Okay, ready?" she asked.

"Yep."

For all his fussing, the kid was quick at least.

"Let's go."

He trotted along, following her as she jogged down to the swamp where she'd hidden her ship.

The Whistle hadn't been a modern model when she'd bought it seven years ago; now, it was dreadfully outdated, but it ran. She'd kept her fueled up just in case. It seemed she was fated to have the most powerful male in their sector looking for her.

"Come on. In."

"Where are we even going?" the boy moaned as the trapdoor closed behind them.

She ruffled his wavy hair. He could moan as much as he wanted today. He was alive. That was all that mattered.

"I'll let you know when we get there."

"Who was that officer? He wore a white uniform. I've never seen one like that. Looked so cool!"

"I doubt it was a uniform."

"Well, it wasn't an exosuit, but it was cut like the—"

"Get your stuff in your cabin and meet me in command. I need a copilot."

He was too busy yelling in delight to keep talking of Kai. Good thing, too. Nalini couldn't bear to think of him right now. If she could help it, she'd never think of him again.

She fired up the Whistle before opening up a holographic map of the galaxy. The known universe lit up in blue, calculating routes from her location to any of the inhabitable planets. There were so many. Millions of planets, hundreds of thousands of systems. She could go anywhere. She wanted to run to the end of the galaxy.

Hands shaking, Nalini opened up the Ratna Belt. Nine systems. Thirty planets.

Kai had found her on Itri. He'd guess that she'd pick another hideout like her small village next. That was her first instinct, but she repressed it. Instead, she pulled up the very last system where anyone would think to look for her.

"Vratis?"

Kronos was quick.

"We're going to *Vratis*?" half incredulous, half ecstatic, the boy yelled, "Wicked!"

She quickly ran through the job calls recently sent through the most boring parts of the system.

"Don't get excited. We're headed to Maul, in the farisles, east of the torrent. They're calling for cargo transporters. At least this old bucket of rust is big enough for that. But that's pretty quiet."

"And still a hundred million times better than Fruja," he argued.

The boy wasn't wrong. She pulled up the job, and commed in to the station noted as the job coordinator. No one really applied as a transporter; they didn't need qualifications, just a decent ship with enough room for the load. Thieves knew better than to attempt to take official cargos; they generally had trackers hidden inside the load.

As long as no one had called before her, the job would be hers. As it had only been posted a few minutes ago, she had a fair chance of getting it.

Surprisingly, the communication, went through.

"Nali Black of The Whistle, a Cn-1771," she introduced herself, "answering call 471 in the Ratna database. You need pilots, I hear?"

She didn't expect an immediate answer; who knew what time it was over there? She hadn't checked.

"Warris Bair of Maul, Vratis. Damn, a Cn? Are they even making those anymore?"

"Not these last two decades, I don't think. If she's

suitable for what you need, I'll head over to your post right now."

"She'll do. We're just trying to move belongings, and people, from this sector to the Empire. With what's happening, bunch of folks have started to migrate. Great time to get into real estate, if you ask me."

Nalini hesitated. Did she want to go anywhere near the Imperials at all?

But at least, Imperials weren't actively looking for her.

"I'll be there at 0612 according to my flight plan. Clearance codes would help."

"You got it, Whistle. Bair, out."

She stopped the communication, removed the comm device at her jaw, and passed over a series of numbers to Kronos.

"There, enter the coordinates."

She purposefully left him to it without hovering; checking after his work in a few minutes wouldn't hurt. The kid did good, entering each number accurately. Good thing, too, or they might have found themselves at the other end of the galaxy.

"What's next?" she asked.

Kronos's little face crunched up in concentration,

then he activated all their shields, their artificial gravity, and air dispensers before saying, "Time for warp."

Nali smiled, grateful for the distraction. She undid her belt and got up from the captain's chair. "Come on, you do it. You've earned it."

The boy seamlessly got their ship to light speed.

Now that they were safely on their way, reality hit like a thousand punches. Suddenly, she was very, very tired. And just as afraid to sleep.

"Well done. You wanna go get some rest? We'll have to pass through customs in five hours."

"Okay, but wake me up for landing!"

"I promise."

They weren't an affectionate pair, but she still pulled him to her as he passed her by. He didn't even complain.

Too soon, though, he was gone, and she was alone.

Truly alone.

She'd shut the connection, that bond, that link that had been so much of a constant it was almost a part of her. Now there was a wall firmly in place between Kai and her. For good reasons.

SHE WAS AFRAID. Petrified. Not because of what

Kai's enforcer had done to Kronos, although that would have been enough to make just about anyone panic. Not because she'd seen Kai bring the child back to life, an impossibility which made it clear just how powerful the male really was.

She was afraid because the moment when their hands touched, she'd finally seen it. The future, and the past that had eluded her for over a decade. The reasons why she had been inherently terrified of him from the start.

She'd seen it as clearly as she saw the console flashing before her eyes to indicate that their sensor didn't discern any threat ahead.

The goldish, misty matter created out of nowhere by Kai's hand. She'd seen it destroy ships. Thousands of ships, gone after one single deadly blow.

It was Starfire. She'd touched it. Felt it. Tonight it had been soft and warm, unthreatening, and used for good. Used to ignite a spark in the broken, lifeless body of a boy.

But her vision showed a cloaked creature—a woman, she thought—using it in the past, lighting up the skies and crushing all those ships into nothing. And then, clearly, she saw it again, used by Kai, this time. Against a star.

He would destroy a *star*.

That wouldn't have petrified her as much, had she not seen herself standing right next to him.

No. That wasn't who she was. She couldn't be.

Nalini wasn't one to turn her nose up at those who killed to live. That simple equation, she understood. In this world, sometimes one had to pull the trigger to survive. She could live with the guilt of ending a life for self-preservation. Most people did it every day when they ate another living organism to survive. But destroying a *star*? Condemning an entire system— various planets, everyone and everything on them?

She closed her eyes.

It wasn't going to happen. It just wasn't.

But how often had her clear, specific visions been wrong?

EIGHTEEN

AN OLD MAN

Piloting cargo was boring, but it paid well, well enough for them to be able to get a place within a month; good thing, too, as sleeping in the Whistle blew. That leaky old thing smelled damp.

Nalini returned to her habits soon, growing her plants and making a mess in the lounge. Adaptable as ever, Kronos found simulation games to amuse himself.

The one thing that truly changed was the sense of Kai's presence. For years, she'd felt it there, but it had seemed entirely ignorant of her. Now, it watched. Listened. She was sure that if she ever reached into it, so much as said his name, he'd be there.

She never did.

One day, at the market, she saw it. The most beautiful beast she'd ever seen; white and blue fur, a presence that was entirely out of place around people. It was huge, close to the size of a pony. The wolf didn't snap his jaw at anyone, but it certainly acted like it wanted to.

Unable to resist the desire to greet the magnificent creature, Nalini remained still and held out her hand, inviting him to check it out.

"Hello, handsome one," she called.

The beast approached slowly and sniffed. Then it huffed, but, as it didn't snap its jaw, she took it as a win.

"Well, look at this!"

She lifted her gaze and immediately tensed, her smile disappearing. She knew that man.

He was in his prime, with salt and pepper hair and a well-trimmed beard. His imposing frame, working hands, sun-kissed skin, and common cloak didn't fool her.

She'd never seen him before. But she *knew him*. Who —what—he was.

"I know how to use my blaster and my knife," she practically growled, low and threateningly.

They were in public, so there was a chance that he might not mean to make a scene.

Right?

"No doubt, little lady."

She froze and glared. Only one person had ever called her that, although she was, in fact, quite short for an Evris.

"Where are my manners. Ian Krane," he introduced himself, offering his hand in greeting.

She looked at it like he might keep a venomous snake in his sleeve.

"I don't bite, Nalini."

Each word coming out of his mouth made things a hundred times worse. He knew her? Her name. Her location.

"Why don't we go speak somewhere, hmm?"

"*Speak*," she spat. "When your kind would have us all dead?"

"I don't speak for the Council, child."

"But you're a Wise."

The male didn't deny it, shrugging. "Don't hold it against me. You hang out with crazies for a mere hundred years and peeps will associate you with them for a damn millennium."

Still frowning, and mistrusting, Nalini shook the man's hand. She looked around, searching for his backup, but no one she could see or sense in the market seemed to pay them any mind. Except the beast.

"Is he yours?" she asked, pointing to the wolf, who she would have sworn seemed to raise a brow, piqued at the idea.

"Hardly. These beasts don't belong to anyone. But he hangs out with me right now, yeah. We were looking for you. Took us a while to get your trail. Which is saying a lot." The male tapped his own temple. "I ain't all that bad at seeing things myself."

Nalini was a little lost; she didn't feel animosity coming from Ian Krane, and if he meant to subdue her, he hadn't brought any weapon to do so. She adjusted her stance as to not look like she was about to pounce or flee, all the while remaining careful, wary of the strange old mage.

"Why were you looking for me?"

"You know," he said, not immediately answering her question, "back in the day, we had classes for kids like you. Show you how to distinguish past, possible futures, and actual, unchangeable prophecies. Otherwise, it can get pretty jumbled up in your head. A little scary, too. Makes some of us paranoid. Others go mad."

She glared and stayed silent.

"Not saying you should trust me. You shouldn't. I have my own agenda. Just saying, I know a thing or ten, and you need help if you want to make it to thirty before going completely bonkers. I could teach you."

Nalini might have loved hearing that ten years ago.

Might.

"Why would you want to help?"

"I don't," he point-blank stated. "Not really. But I need to. I live in this galaxy, and the fate of it depends on one big boy we both know. There's one person in this entire universe who can make sure he doesn't destroy it. One girl who wastes her time transporting crap and doesn't practice her skills. So, yeah, I'd say that's my problem."

She looked around frantically, checking whether anyone was hearing a word of what they were saying. She should have listened for once, and spoken to him in private. But no one was paying attention to an irrelevant cargo pilot and an old man.

"You know Kai."

"You could say that, kid."

She sighed. "Well, as a Wise, you probably know exactly what he is. No one can control him, let alone me. I just see stuff. He's about a million times stronger than me."

She wasn't a bad psychic, and she could take care of herself, but she wasn't deluding herself into thinking that she'd ever be strong enough to take Kai on, even if she'd wanted to. Twelve years ago, maybe – not now.

"Darkness reborn, yada, yada. Yeah, I know the prophecy. Probably a little better than you, given the fact that I freaking wrote it."

She froze. Then, she had to ask, "Are you insane?"

The older male laughed and held his hand up again.

"I'm sane enough for this. Come with me."

"Sorry, but I don't do politics. I have zero interest in fighting against, or for, Kai, for that matter. I just want to live my life in peace."

And if that made her a coward, so be it.

Krane carried on his pitch, like she hadn't even spoken. "You can bring the boy. You know you're meant for more than this, kiddo. Someone like you shouldn't spend her life transporting crap in a stinking ship."

She crossed her arms on her chest.

"It pays."

The old male sighed. "For the sake of everything holy in the universe, *I'll pay you* to get some training. Happy?"

"No."

She started walking away, done with this conversation. She wasn't getting herself pulled into this.

"Nalini," the male called her back.

She sighed and turned.

"What now?"

"I can guarantee that I'd never even attempt to make you fight anyone's war. I'm just a damn seer who *knows* how this story ends if you can't take care of yourself."

She had to consider it, feeling her resolve falter. She didn't know her future. He was implying that it wasn't all that good.

"You basically told me not to trust you. And I don't. Why should I listen to a word you're saying?"

"Because you want to remain sane, and safe. Because you're curious about getting some actual training by someone who knows what he's talking about. And, mostly, because your job bores you to tears and you'd literally eat your own leg rather than doing it for the rest of your life."

Damn old psychic male.

"I'm not leaving with a *Wise* without any sort of guarantee or proof that you won't just dump us in a ditch and set it on fire."

Ian Krane nodded. "Smart girl."

He removed the gray glove covering his hand before extending it again; after a beat, she took it, knowing he meant it as more than a greeting this time.

When their palms touched, she investigated his mind. The process could be painful for both parties when the subject was strong enough to resist, and there was no doubt that Ian would have been strong enough, but he'd lowered his mental shield. He let her read him. His intentions. His thoughts. His feelings.

He was still shielding part of him—his past, the deeper part of his thoughts—but the rest was laid bare, proving that he'd meant every word he'd said. He let her see the future he saw. Her deaths. By fire, an exploding space ship, screaming on the ground. Three times, she saw her death; she didn't look much older in any of those visions.

Shit.

Nalini's resolve straightened. She was going with him. The moment she decided that, the future changed. She was in a colorful garden. In front of a waterfall. Dancing in the street. Laughing.

She was alive.

Through his mind, she also saw what he intended for

her. What he was really offering. She gasped and let his hand go.

"So, what do you think?" he asked.

She stared, entirely incredulous.

"Is that possible? I didn't think anyone *could* go there. It's warded and unmappable."

Ian shot her a smile that showed all of his teeth.

"You said it yourself, girl. I'm a Wise. And whether they like it or not, as a member of the Council, I can do what I damn well please."

She blinked.

"What do you say, kiddo?"

There was only one thing to say.

"I'll start packing."

Kronos wasn't hard to convince either. A few hours later, he and Nalini were trailing the Zonian in the Whistle, en route for Tejen, the mythic original planet their entire race came from.

KAI HAD CONQUERED HAIMO EARLY, making it one of the first systems he'd annexed. Not for sentimental reasons; he'd simply believed that owning those forges, which didn't have any equal in the Ratna Belt, and the treasures of the mineral planet, would give him a strategic advantage.

He'd been right.

A few surprises had awaited him. He'd genuinely believed that after all these years, most of those he had known would have died. Most slaves didn't live past their forties. But Mae was still alive, so was Balu, his uncle Isha, and even that suborn old Kumi. She was blind, and mostly bedridden, but she still made the best drinks when she was able to be up and around.

They all regarded him with fear and suspicion; he couldn't blame them. The vibe he emanated wasn't ever friendly. Particularly not toward those who'd let him die in the cold.

Most of the workmasters died in their short, pathetic offensive against his forces. The Hora surrendered after five days of siege. Akia accepted the demand to free the slaves and waited to hear his fate, no doubt expecting a death sentence. But Kai was utterly indifferent. He hadn't reclaimed this world to exert his vengeance upon his past. His past was irrelevant. Only the future mattered to him.

"You'll supply my armies with the weapons they need. We will pay fairly. A fair salary *will* be distributed amongst the workers. Some of my men will remain here. If I hear that you returned to your old ways, I'll take pleasure in signing your execution warrant," he told the male who'd fathered him.

Speaking to his mother was... difficult. She was glad to see him, he could tell. She cried tears of joy and said things that should have moved his cold heart.

They didn't.

Mae had given him life and cared for him as best she could, so he attempted to feel some sort of kinship toward her, but failed.

The wolves liked it back here. Space was cold, but whenever he'd been grounded on any planet, they'd struggled in the heat. Perhaps that was one of the reasons why Kai spent most of his time in space; to ensure his pack was comfortable.

Kai watched them play in the snow and found himself smiling. His smile stilled quickly. They were always fleeting.

HE'D RETURNED to Haimo periodically over the years. Wench joked it was for Kumi's beverage, and he wasn't entirely wrong; but it became his escape because of the forge.

Isha had the complete run of the place without any interference from overlords in there now. The male kept Kai's old work station empty, as he turned up without warning from time to time.

Only popping by for a day at a time when he had a chance, Kai had taken months to create weapons that fitted him perfectly—deer horn knives made of fyriron and energy. No one else could use them; they were just hilts until he pushed his power through them. Then, curved blades of energy-coated fyriron appeared out of the hilt. He'd let others attempt to activate the weapon, and all had failed; the hilts only reacted to his specific energy. He liked that, a lot.

They were beauties. Wench had moaned and groaned until Kai caved and made him an axe designed the same way. Working at the forge was therapeutic; he generally went there without a clear goal in mind. He'd also ended up forging weapons for his most loyal supporters, Hart, Star, Evi, Park, and Ollis. Some of his other creations, he'd just left behind in the forge. They'd be sold to someone, some-where. He didn't care.

Today was different. He knew what he was doing when he formed the long, slim hilt, which would be perfectly comfortable in a small hand. He carved it with care and encrusted it with red crystals.

"This won't be stable," Isha frowned, watching over his shoulder. "Whatever blade you fit in there will be shot through with too much energy for any man."

Kai shrugged. "It's not for a man." It was for a goddess who'd hold it without flinching. "And it's not a blade, either." He lifted the long tress of carefully braided fyriron strands.

Isha winced. "A whip."

No ex-slaves liked those. The whip represented their master's power over them. Which was why it was so extremely perfect for the female who owned him.

He shrugged. "Girls like whips."

Isha wrinkled his nose. "You know some strange girls."

The old master waved toward the weapon. "I'd use a black diamond as an activator. Girls *definitely* like diamonds."

Kai laughed and removed the crystals. His uncle did have a point there.

Kai wore that whip at his belt every day for the next imperial year. Until they met again.

Forest more abundant and rich than anything she'd ever seen; waterfalls so blue and pure she could stand underneath them for hours. The air. The sky. The dragons.

This was paradise.

The first day off from training, Nalini headed straight to the wild gardens and spent her time in there, breathing, smelling, just *being*. One could grow old in peace in these lands.

Peace. It had been a while since she'd felt like it was an achievable concept. And once she reached it, she felt him.

Kai.

She'd believed she'd closed her mind off against him

after Itri, to avoid any communication between them, and prevent him from showing up, but there he was, right in front of her in her mind. Dammit. Too taken by her contemplation, she'd dropped her wall and let him in.

"Nalini."

Her name came out softly.

"Akai."

He looked around, a frown marring his features.

"Where are we?"

She had to roll her eyes. "I thought I'd made it clear I wasn't going to share my whereabouts just because you asked."

"I know this place. This garden." He seemed confused and, for one moment, vulnerable. "There's a palace north of here. Close."

There was.

Then his attention focused on her again.

"No matter. Just give me your coordinates. I have to find you."

Her eyes cut to his. "Have you stopped murdering, burning cities, and demanding obedience in all things of late?" she asked rhetorically.

"I demand they stop killing children. I demand they stop using slaves."

She wasn't petty enough to mention Kronos, although his name hung between them.

"And when they don't immediately fold to your will, you slaughter them."

He titled his head. "Yes. Yes, I do."

Kai kept staring at her, those dark eyes burning into her mind. Probing it. Pushing against it. He was strong enough to obliterate all her barriers, she felt it. But she pushed back, stubbornly.

When the mental fight started to hurt her, he released his hold.

"You don't belong here," he told her, using the knowledge he'd managed to see in her mind. "You're trying to fit in, but you just aren't."

"I don't belong anywhere."

The way he looked at her would have made a lesser female beg for mercy, or break eye contact, at least. She took it full force.

"You belong with me. Pretending otherwise is offensive. Don't insult me again, Nalini."

She snorted. "I don't know what I've done to make you think you could throw your dominance at me,

Kai, I really don't. But let's get something straight right now. Talk to me like you expect me to heel again, and I'll drop by wherever you're hiding in the galaxy and kick your ass into next year."

Her threat amused him. His expression didn't change much, but he might as well have said, *"Aren't you cute, thinking you can intimidate me."*

Asshole.

"It's bigger than you think. The Belt isn't safe right now, Nalini. I'll do my utmost to protect all of my systems from the storm coming, but if you keep on gallivanting Goddess Light knows where, you might get hurt. You saved my life. I owe you. Let me protect you."

She inclined her head.

"And when that imaginary, and rather alarmist danger passes, what then?" she challenged.

He ignored that question. "Come with me."

Why was it still so tempting, despite everything? Was it his voice, his eyes, or the raw need she saw behind it all?

She averted her eyes. "I can't."

And with some effort, she managed to shove a wall between them, shutting off their connection.

Her beautiful sanctuary in the gardens was now

violated by his presence. If she stood there again, she'd think of him. Nalini walked away, heading toward the city, seeking any form of distraction she could find.

Nalini stopped by a little shop with an open window; inside, there was a male with a stern brow, bent over the tanned, exposed skin of a large warrior.

She'd seen that most of the males and females of Tejen bore beautiful marks on their skins, drawings that seemed to tell a story.

She went in, and an assistant came to greet her, explaining the process and showing her the sort of designs the artist could tattoo on her skin.

"This is traditional and a little painful. Androids can mark you with lasers now, you wouldn't feel a thing. But the warriors still get it done with needles."

"I'm not afraid of a little pain," Nalini confessed.

Pain was... distracting. She could use some of that right now.

She waited her turn. When the artist asked what she had in mind, she shrugged. "I just want something around this scar." She showed the ugly mark on her arm and shoulder.

"It's an important scar," the artist guessed. "Beautiful to you."

She nodded.

It marked the day she'd left one warlord. Fitting, on the day she'd just shut another one out, that she highlighted it with decorative tattoos.

"Let's make it beautiful to the rest of the world then."

Kai liked the new bridge of his command ship. It was an oval room, large enough to fit an entire squadron of enforcers. The floor was made of humongous triangular metallic plates. The captain's seat was quite similar to his throne on Vratis, a rectangular block with command platforms either side of its arms - except it was blood red. The rest of the room was an immaculate white.

He'd had that ship built from scratch, a long endeavor that had proved fruitful. As warlord, there were few occasions of using the Lotus in an official capacity. The Dominion made a statement. It also served another purpose. The command ship was large and equipped with so many facilities its crew and passengers could live there for the rest of their lives if they so wished. It could comfortably house a million people, and uncomfortably transport up to seven million for a time. There was no denying that his enemies had grown bolder over the last few months. Better equipped, too. He had every reason to suspect that they had the support of influential groups around the entire galaxy. Perhaps even the Imperials, although the delegation of Coats sent by the emperor had greeted Kai with respect.

This ship helped with his peace of mind. If the need arose, he could evacuate his people from any base relatively fast and safely. The shields Wench and the rest of his team had built had been forged like the shield around Vratis, blending magic with technology. No weapon could penetrate it, not even anything the Imperials had in their possession.

It was the first time he'd made use of the Dominion. She flew well, faster than expected for a baby of her size and weight.

"You surpassed yourself," he told Wench, who beamed.

At his side, Evi rolled her eyes. The female had taken an important place at his side over the last few years, and even more so since they'd conquered Vratis.

There was much to the warlord thing—a lot of politics and endless meetings—and his armies had needed a leader entirely focused on it. He'd named Evi without hesitation. Not only because she was bloodthirsty, but because whatever mission he sent her on, regardless of how dangerous it was, she always brought back her entire team. Sometimes, she lost the battle. She never lost a life.

She'd proved herself a better strategist than Kai, subtler, for one.

When he was on board, he still officially led the fleet, but his general made most of the decisions, only coming to him when she was unsure. Which had happened exactly twice.

He... liked her.

Evi was the first person he'd let in. He'd considered taking her to bed when they'd first met—Goddess knew she was appealing enough—but he'd decided against it. Once he fucked a woman, he was done with her. He liked to stay entirely detached; Evi was too important to compromise their relationship that way.

He also started to trust Wench more, noticing that the little boy had turned into an adult male at some point. Young and enthusiastic, but Kai enjoyed his company.

Kai didn't fail to notice the timing. The ability to feel and let people around him affect him had been entirely foreign to him until recently. Until he'd seen her. Touched her. Her hand. Felt her energy, her power, her love for all things.

Nalini Nova. The female meant for him.

It had been a year since their last meeting. He wondered if she hated him still.

Since that day, he'd played and replayed each of their meetings in his mind. As time passed, he cringed more each time he thought of them.

"*Why?*" she'd asked. Why did he want her? He recalled her eyes when those words crossed her lips. And then, that look when he replied the most stupid thing he could have told her. "*Because you belong here.*"

Here. In his cold Vratisian palace. A place she'd been imprisoned, tortured.

Her eyes when he'd said that. He couldn't stop seeing them, seeing the light leave. Her lip had trembled ever so slightly. She'd taken a step back.

He wouldn't make that mistake again next time he saw her. And there would be a next time.

SHE WAS GOING to kill the old male someday, and she'd laugh with glee while his entrails spilled out of his stomach.

"Taking a break?" Ian Krane asked, one brow raised. "I said twelve laps. You're at ten, if I'm not mistaken."

The stadium she was meant to run around was twenty-four miles in circumference. She'd asked. And then she'd demanded to know if he was insane when he'd demanded that she run it three times *before* they started training.

That was a year ago. Now, they were at twelve times.

She hated running. With all her little heart.

Krane was, no need to say, leisurely lounging on the side of the track, a book in hand.

Asshole.

She picked up her speed, knowing that if she just jogged around slow like this, he'd demand another lap when she was done. If she was going slower than Nox, who loved to tag along, she was too slow for him.

What really blew was the fact that his stupid-ass, cruel method worked. Her first month on Tejen, he simply had her exercise, forge her frail body into something else, work on her stamina, and already she felt stronger and more settled. Things that had required her concentration before, like moving an object with her mind, came with ease.

After the run, he'd had her training in combat with some of the Tejen natives—Evris who rode dragons for fun and started wrestling before they could walk.

She basically spent a week eating dust, crying, and

cursing the name Ian Krane. A year later, she was still eating dust, because, again, her adversaries were that badass. But occasionally, she managed to hold her own—when they were having a bad day or, more than likely, letting her win out of pity.

The real work had started the second month. She understood now how fucking pointless that cage and the shocks of energy coursing through her body had really been. It was not training, just torture.

Training a seer took quiet, peace, and nature. Sitting in silence while listening to the water and extending her mind to it. Seeing it. Predicting its current. Knowing which fish would eat the other one. And then, in the middle of all that, when she was really one with everything around her, Krane hit her with a stick. A simple slap on her hand, not meant to hurt at all. Just... training.

It wasn't easy because Krane was forcing her to catch glimpses of the future that involved *her*. Her power was designed to look outward, glance far and wide. After two weeks, she knew when to move her hand to avoid those hits. The following month, instead of a peaceful beach, she was to do the same in a forest full of predators and prey, where nature was busier and more dangerous. It wasn't Krane and a stick inter-rupting her then; it was tigers and dragons. She had to avoid their claws or die.

She was still alive, so something must have worked.

The third month, Krane announced, "I think you're strong enough now. We can get started."

"What were the last ninety days all about then?" She rolled her eyes.

He grinned. "Making sure you don't break."

That had made little sense to her at the time. Later that day, crying out in pain, she understood.

"There's exactly two reasons why we're here. The first one is so that you can read these. No one is allowed to take them off-planet or copy them," Krane said, pointing to the bunch of books he'd placed right in front of her. "And the second one is to train your mind to push against invasion. *Any* invasion. Even as you sleep, I need you to keep it closed."

And so, the torment had begun.

"Resist me."

But she couldn't. Krane pushed her mind relentlessly, breaching it. Her nose bled, her every muscle ached.

Reading the books wasn't much better. They were boring. *Boring*. All had one common denominator: information on psychic bonds. Bonds between mothers and children from the womb. Bonds between wives and husbands. Bonds between friends.

Basically, people were happier when they had a link to someone else. Yay. Great information.

What she would have given for a good old thriller instead.

KRONOS HAD classes that didn't involve fighting off firebreathers, being psychologically raped on a regular basis, or boring books. Lucky kid.

Still, despite the insane, intense training, Nalini was strangely... happy here. People accepted her. No judgment, no fear, no threat.

There were mages on Tejen. That shocked her; they weren't killed and hunted like the rest of their kind elsewhere in the galaxy.

Those born with powers were directly overseen by the order of the Wise.

"I don't get it. Your Council makes the whole galaxy destroy us everywhere – and here, it's fine?"

Krane sighed. "Each mage born here passes various tests that ensured that they aren't Darkness, as soon as their powers manifest themselves. It isn't doable on a larger scale. Here, there's a maximum of half a dozen mages born each year on the whole planet. We can handle it. I'm not saying the Council made the right decision when they opted to condemn every child with magic, but we certainly couldn't have trained them all throughout the galaxy like we do here."

She agreed begrudgingly: the Wise trained youth on a one-on-one basis. As there were less than two hundred of them in their order, they certainly couldn't have overseen the entire universe. But Ian was right, that didn't excuse the Council's edict. In her opinion there just was no valid reason for killing children.

THE COUNCIL HAD little weight on that planet, ruled by its own warlord, a female who welcomed Nalini with open arms. Rani Tharshen wielded magic herself.

"Seers are very rare," she said. "Although perhaps not in your family."

An ugly, old wound reared its head at the mention of her family. Nalini brushed it aside every time it flared.

"You've missed the solstice," the warlord had said, welcoming her when they arrived. "It was just yesterday."

Nalini saw Krane tense behind her. "Perhaps it's not such a bad thing. We don't celebrate those things out there," he pointed upward, toward the skies.

Rani had smiled wickedly. "Well, that should be a treat to you both next year."

The old male twitched. As soon as the ruler had disappeared, he warned Nalini, "Don't ask. And we're getting out of here before the year is out. You don't want to see a winter solstice here. Trust me on this."

It had been a year, now, and the solstice was tomorrow. They were supposed to leave today. This was her last training day here. Soon, they'd be back to the real world—their real world, at least, outside of this wonderland bathed in sunlight.

She mostly thought he was talking out of his ass and doing his best to avoid the solstice for some reason, which only served to make her more curious about it. She'd attended various events throughout the year, and damn, they could party here. She'd even learned to dance, unable to resist the music, the sea of bodies undulating with each beat getting under her skin.

How different could it be?

"Very," he'd replied, when she asked just that.

Which wasn't a response at all, so she'd gone to ask someone else.

People just giggled and blushed when she mentioned the ceremony, telling her frustrating things like, "You'll see" and "Don't miss it."

She'd argued all month about attending. Krane was adamant that they shouldn't. But as she happened to be a twenty-five-year-old, grown-ass female, she declared, "Fine, you can go if you're in a rush. Give me coordinates, and I'll catch up. *I'm staying.*"

"That's a fucking *no*. Trust me on this, dammit."

"You told me not to trust you once. I listened."

He wasn't giving in, so she'd done the one thing anyone would have and disabled his ship's hyperdrive. Goddess Light knew it would take the old male more than a day to figure out what was wrong with his ship.

TWENTY-ONE
SOLSTICE

She should have flown far, far away from here.

"What's happening to me?" Nalini cried, throwing up in the toilet for the sixth time since she'd woken up an hour ago.

The contents of her stomach just wouldn't stay in, but that was nothing compared to the headache and the way her muscles ached, feeling heavy.

Krane smirked, filing his nails. "I'd say you reap what you sow, or something of the sort, if you didn't look quite so miserable." Then he beamed. "Want something to drink? Won't help, but, hey, might as well stay hydrated."

She crawled to her bed, feeling like she was going to die.

"Hope you're enjoying the solstice, by the way."

She really, really wanted to ask what any of this had to do with the solstice, but Krane was already feeling way too smug.

Kronos pressed a cold compress to her head. That helped for all of three seconds.

Finally, she gave in. "What's wrong with me?"

"You mean, other than a stubborn streak and too many skills with a wrench? Nothing at all."

She glared with as much hostility as she could muster.

"That might work better if you didn't look like a puppy drowned in sweat."

Krane caved. "Go to the kitchen," he told Kronos, "and ask them to make a tea for your sister. They know what she needs."

Once the child had left, he turned to her, still looking quite smug. "This," said he, "is the start of a millennia-old ceremony celebrated by our kind here. You, and every unattached youth with magic who are currently of age, are giving your power to nature, feeding it for the next year. And once you're truly, completely depleted, you're going to have to replenish it. That's where the party starts. Fear not. The most attractive volunteers, male and female, will be gathered at the festivities tonight. And you will take them, many of them, feeding like one of the beasts we once were."

She watched him with undiluted horror. "I'll *eat* people!"

He laughed hard, slapping his leg. "Goddess Light help you, sweet summer child. No, little lady. You're gonna fuck people. Enjoy your solstice."

She stared. Then, whatever was left in her stomach came out right there in her bed.

Eating people might not have been as bad.

Krane explained things to her as she basked in misery, torment, and regret. Talks of energy, replenishing it. Harnessing, he called it. Causing orgasms and feeding off them.

"Why didn't you drag me out of here."

A kinder person would have said nothing, but Krane shrugged. "Tried, sugar. You made us stay. Maybe you'll listen next time."

Kronos came back with a strange brew that smelled like feet, but, after drinking it, she managed to fall into a deep, dreamless slumber.

When she woke, the sickness had receded some. Her limbs were still weak. So was her mind.

She recalled wishing her powers away in her youth. Wishing that she wasn't different from other girls out there, just a regular without the visions, the energy. They said be careful what you wish for. She *hated* it. Truly abhorred being so crippled, broken, vulnerable.

Someone had changed her soiled sheets and cleaned her up sometime while she slept. They'd also left a dress hanging in her bathroom.

Well, if she could call this a dress at all. It was nothing but triangular patches of cloth tied together in the middle, baring the sides of her tummy, and most of her legs, barely holding her breasts.

She winced at her reflection. Everyone else would be wearing the same thing, no doubt; whatever outfit had been laid out for her before a feast fit in with the dress code.

Tonight was about one thing, and they weren't bothering to hide it.

Nalini was no untouched flower. She'd developed an interest in males pretty late, granted, but she'd done something about it. Touching herself, thinking of the dark eyes of a powerful male she'd met once in her entire life—and okay, seen another couple of times through weird, and weirdly realistic, visions—was too pathetic for words. So, she'd just pulled an attractive warrior who had been looking at her *that* way into her room soon after her arrival here.

Baz. She'd played with him a handful of times since, when the itch needed scratching. She was leaving, and neither of them were even remotely attached, so they could simply have some harmless fun. He knew what to do with all his body parts, so he served a purpose. She wasn't against casual sex, but this, this backward, forced fornication no one had even warned her about, was different.

Frustrated and angry—at Krane and everyone else, for not spelling things out properly, but mostly at herself—she burst out of her room and raced down to the party, intending to find Baz and get it over with.

She froze in the great hall.

There was only one city planet-wide, and everyone in it liked to meet for one reason or another once a week at least, so the palace they'd built was of an adequate size. Humongous. And right now, it was entirely filled with naked people. Cocks. Cocks everywhere. And pussies, too, but those were a little less conspicuous.

Only mages were dressed, if the outfits they wore, similar to Nalini's, could even be called that.

"Nalini, dear."

She closed her mouth and counted to ten in her mind as Rani Tharshen greeted her, taking her forearm.

"Warlord," she managed to say without yelling, and not even adding one single insult.

"Your first solstice. I don't think I've ever witnessed so

much energy entering the planet. We're blessed to have you," she said, pulling her forward.

"You..." She cleared her throat. "Participate?"

"Oh, yes. I'm not attached," Rani replied, winking. "And there's something quite exhilarating in these bestial nights. Come, let us go choose our partners."

Plural. Krane had already said something of the sort. She winced. "I was going to try to find a guy I know— Baz..." She struggled to remember the name he'd given her on their first meeting. "Uaani."

Rani laughed. "A good boy, for sure. He won't do the trick, not tonight. You'd need a dozen like him to return to your full health. No, let me help; I've sampled quite a few of the pickings."

Never mind feeling better, she was going to be sick again all over the warlord's cut-out robes.

"I can't—" She winced. "—sleep with a bunch of strangers out of the blue."

Rani tilted her head, as though trying to understand what she'd said at all. Then she patted her hand, not without kindness.

"I forgot. It has been a long time since my first solstice. Centuries. It's very strange to a young girl."

At least someone made sense. Although at twenty-five, she wasn't as young as the warlord made her feel when she said that.

Still, compared to a female who'd seen centuries, she supposed she was.

"Your misgivings, forget them. You'll take many men through the night."

She hadn't believed it at the time. But finally, she found Baz and dragged him to her room as fast as her poor limbs would carry her. She knelt in front of him and took his length in her mouth, making him hiss in pleasure. Krane had said it was about taking their energy after release; she needed it now. Nalini wasn't the obedient type. She didn't feel like actually having sex with anyone, so that seemed like the best course of action. She worked him up with her tongue, and, after five minutes, the warrior exploded in her mouth.

Nalini froze, the most delicious, addictive rush of power coursing through her body, making her tremble in ecstasy, not unlike an orgasm of her own.

It didn't last. The next second, it had passed, and she still felt depleted. Hungry.

That night, she learned to do as she was told, sometimes. And she enjoyed it.

They left on the morrow, after she'd repaired their hyperdrive. She'd never tell Krane, but now that it was all over and done with, she was glad that she'd disobeyed. Glad of that wild night with five males, and glad of knowing herself a little more. She'd always been a little shy with males, not quite confident. No more.

The real challenge would be not imaging a certain pair of eyes when she closed her eyes during sex. Someday, she might manage. It was always so damn awkward as soon as she opened her eyes again, and found the wrong person below her.

"Where to now?" she asked.

"I," Krane replied, "am going to the Council. You're heading to Nimeria."

"Nimeria," she repeated, frowning.

"Aye. Enlil's loyalists have a base there, and they're recruiting for simple hands. You could even go back to loading cargo." He winked. She frowned some more.

What was the point of the last year if he just wanted her to go back to doing what she'd been doing then? And for loyalists, too. That made no freaking sense. She didn't feel one way or another about the group that had rallied against Kai, but she knew Krane had no love for them.

Still, she gave the old male the benefit of the doubt. He'd led her right so far.

"If it would do any good, I'd say come with me. I'm going to be right in a viper's nest, and I could use an ally. But Nalini, you'd be a hindrance."

Well, that hurt.

He further explained, "You aren't interested in politics, in the greater good, and anything like that."

She couldn't exactly protest: he had a point there. She just hadn't realized he was completely done with her.

"You've shut yourself off from the rest of the world since you were seventeen, Nalini. You hid where you wouldn't see what either side is doing. You don't know the first thing about Kai Lor Hora, or his enemies. So, go to the loyalist base. Keep your head down. Observe. Make up your own mind. When the time is right, you can decide for yourself where you want to stand in this war."

"I don't want to be in a war at all."

He seemed downright exasperated. "Nalini, I like you, kiddo. A lot. So it's with a lot of affection that I'm saying this. The entire galaxy is at war, and you're gonna get pulled in someday, however far you ran. Continue fleeing from the shadow of a dead man, until you get kidnapped, killed, or worse. Grow the fuck up. Enlil is gone. He isn't after you anymore."

"But Kai is. He wants my powers, my vision. He wants..."

"You have *no idea* what he wants. And you have no idea what's happening out there."

"I see plenty," she argued.

Krane seemed exasperated by this point. "You see battles, you see deaths, but you don't know why any of it is happening. You can't see the forest for the trees." He sighed. "Remain ignorant and stubborn if you so wish, kiddo. Or be stronger than this, better than this, and go to Nimeria."

Irritated, she glared, but his words ended up hitting the mark as the seconds passed. He was right. She might not like it, but he was right. She had no fucking clue why either side was fighting; for power, she guessed. Beyond that, she was ignorant.

Nalini nodded, slowly agreeing, and Krane smiled, before uncharacteristically pulling her into a very brief hug.

It felt nice. Warm.

"You're in control now," he told her. "Infinitely better at reading what you need to see. You'll see. By Goddess Light, in time, you'll know exactly what you're supposed to do."

She smiled at the older man. "It sounds like a farewell."

"It is." Ian winked. "For now, anyway."

He bent and opened his arms up to Kronos, who also went for a short and highly reluctant hug. He was too cool for hugs.

"You take care of each other, kids."

"Sure," Kronos replied, shrugging. "No one else will."

Nox, who still wasn't sure about Nalini, was good enough to let her stroke him behind the ear before following the Wise Councilmaster into the Zonian. In no time, the ship was flying out.

Nalini was confused by the strength of her own feelings as the male left her behind. She'd never had this before. Someone older, wiser, who was helping her for no other reason that the fact that he cared about her – whatever he said about ulterior motives. And she'd mourn the loss of her friend and mentor.

She wasn't the only one who'd regret leaving.

"I'll miss it here," the teenager mused, stealing a last glance at the beautiful world they were leaving.

Nalini forced herself to speak. "You really can stay, you know."

It was the best thing for him. Staying here, in this place where he was taught better than anywhere else in the world. Where he wouldn't ever be hunted for his magic. But when Rani had offered Kronos a place in her land, the boy had refused.

Nalini was selfish enough to not insist he stay. What was she supposed to do without him?

"Don't be ridiculous. You wouldn't survive a week by yourself. You can't boil water."

She pouted. "You said my last soup was edible."

"I lied. Poured it into a plant pot. The plant died."

NIMERIA WASN'T A BAD PLACE, overall. Nalini

and Kronos might even have been impressed, had they not spent a year in a true paradise. Kronos lamented the absence of dragons, and Nalini wished for more abs and triceps.

The very thought of joining the loyalists, as Krane had suggested, was distasteful to her. He was right; getting involved in any sort of politics went against her every instinct. She woke up in the morning intending to do something about it, and then found a pretext to stay away. Homeschooling Kronos. Tending to her plants. Attempting to cook something that they could eat without grimacing; in this, she always failed.

There was money aplenty in an account bearing her name now; Krane had in fact made good on his word. He paid her for her year away, quite well. As she hadn't had any cause to spend any of it, they were comfortable without her needing to earn their bread. Still, she earned some coin; she couldn't help but notice the female who was always coughing when she passed by her little terrace on her way back from her work each afternoon. One day, Nalini offered her a draft, and each day that weak, at the same hour, she had one ready.

Her long hours with nothing else to do than reading in her youth had paid off; she knew the properties of most plants, and while her garden was an occupation she enjoyed, her practical mind had made her seek plants for their use rather than their esthetic.

Soon, the town whispered of a pretty healer who'd managed to shift Pera's endless cough, where all else had failed for years; they came to her door again, just like they had in Fruja.

That's how, although she never found it in herself to seek out the loyalists, the loyalists came to her.

The tall male who knocked at her door was handsome, and Nalini thought she recognized some of his features, although she would have been hard-pressed to place him. Had she been more intrigued, she might have scanned his mind. She wasn't.

He watched her in a way that didn't quite sit well with her; not just like he liked what he saw; it was as if he also felt entitled to take it if he pleased.

"How can I help?" she asked.

The male explored her small place, ignoring her question, and picking up random things like he had the right to.

"I hear you live here alone with your son."

She could have rolled her eyes. Kronos was thirteen now, and, while she was twenty-five, people often assumed that she was younger because of her small frame and her diminished height compared to other

Evris females. It was the first time anyone had accused her of having born the boy.

"It's just me and Kronos, yes."

He seemed pleased. She was losing patience.

"Is there a point to this interrogation, sir?"

Catching her irritation, the male finally consented to stop putting his paws on her things.

"My apologies. I was sent by Seraka Mayn," he said, like the name was supposed to mean something to her. It sounded vaguely familiar, but Nalini's memory had a tendency to obliterate things she found of little importance.

She blinked. The stranger clarified, "General of the loyalist armies and lord of this system."

Ah, that guy.

"And what could he need with little old me?"

"The general has put a call through for additional troops. We are, amongst other things, looking for healers specifically. We've heard talk of your skills. Given that you've moved to this specific planet recently, we assumed that you may be against the current government."

The male was slowly approaching her, taking detours, zigzagging through the house. If she wasn't a 100 percent certain that she could have mopped the floor with his face with blinders on and one hand tied behind her back, she might have felt threatened. As things stood, he only disgusted her.

Nalini considered her options. She was itching to tell him to go fuck himself, but Krane's words haunted her. He had been right: she didn't know anything of these loyalists. And she knew even less of Kai's rule. Her one brush with it had caused Kronos's death; since then, she'd stayed the fuck away. Staying in her little house, in the village, far from them, wasn't going to suddenly open her eyes.

Ignorance was weakness. So, yes, she'd observe them for a time. Making her own mind up about the things happening in the world wasn't a bad idea.

"Why, yes. I'm positively against the current government," she lied.

She simply knew nothing of it, and it was past time to change that. Looking at it through the eyes of its enemy was step one.

"If you were to join our cause, you'd have to reside in the base, for your safety; it's not far from here. There are training and instructional facilities on base for your child. You'll be well taken care of and paid fairly."

The sleek snake was so close she could smell his cologne now. She'd need to keep her distances from him, or she'd kill him. Slowly.

"Great."

She walked away, heading to her kitchen, and started cleaning up, making it clear she was busy, and putting as much distance between them as she could.

"A transport can pick you up as early as tomorrow."

"That's fine. Well, better get packing."

Nalini wasn't sure if it had been Ian Krane's goal, but by the end of her first week in the Nimerian base, she was ready to enlist with the other side of the conflict. Had he appeared to her right then and asked her to join him, she would have jumped to stand next to Kai.

These males, and the rare few females who followed them, needed killing. Badly. They didn't value lives. Not the lives of anything that wasn't Evris, or the lives of animals or children who didn't have the right name.

There were slaves in the base. *Slaves*. People from other sentient races, like Krarkens and Valuas, as well as Evris who'd been sold to them, or had committed a crime of some sort. Slaves kept in chains, barely fed, rarely allowed to wash, expected to work during their every waking hour. Needless to say, they received no payment for their labor.

Nalini had never seen any slave before that day, not with her own eyes. There had been some in Vratis when Enlil had ruled, but none had been deemed good enough to even step foot in the warlord's palace. She knew slavery was a terrible thing, but she never understood how evil it really was until she saw their eyes, devoid of any hope. Practically devoid of life. Somewhere in her mind, she'd just believed slaves were lower paid workers. A lower class, but not so very different from her. How wrong she'd been.

They worked from dawn to dusk without more than a short break when they were permitted to eat—probably so they didn't faint. It wouldn't do to delay the completion of their jobs, after all.

Their clothing was nothing but rags. Females wore very little at all.

"We can't stay here," Kronos said one night. "You'll kill someone. And I'll help."

She nodded. They needed to go, but it wouldn't be as easy as that. Now that they'd been enrolled, their departure would be seen as defecting. There was no doubt that the vile snake always watching her would make a point of catching her, and, who knew, perhaps put her in chains once he had.

He'd finally introduced himself. Veli Par Hora, he was called.

Nalini had laughed in his face, to his confusion, of course. Kai's brother. Half-brother, in any case. That explained why she vaguely recognized his features. He was slimmer and pastier than Kai, and his face was longer, but there certainly was a similar air. That should have made him attractive, yet the knowledge only made him appear more repulsive to her.

Thankfully for her sanity, she was kept busy. The shitty fighting ships the soldiers piloted had terrible shields, which meant a lot of them came back bruised and burned—or didn't come back at all. They'd gone for a higher number of ships instead of purchasing fewer, safer ones. Of course they had.

Tending to the wounds of these Evris was a bitter-sweet occupation; she'd never met anyone she didn't wish to help. But the cause they'd received these wounds for, that she couldn't support.

She was exploring the natural tunnels in the belly of the cavernous base one day when she felt a presence behind her.

She started, half expecting Veli, who was never far, sniffing around her like a wolf in heat, but it was one of the soldiers she'd patched up a few days earlier.

"Hey. I see the arm is better," she said, pointing to his now bandage-free limb.

"You did good." Heio Su smiled at her. Then he gestured to the tunnel she'd planned to explore. "Don't go that way. We've closed off the entrance, but there're beasts you don't want to see on the other side. Sometimes, they claw some passages through. Takes ten men to put them down."

Nalini lifted a curious brow. "What sort of beasts?"

If he'd meant to scare her, he'd failed. If one didn't take dragons into account, she'd never met an animal whose mind she couldn't control. She couldn't force them to like her, but their simple minds were easily breached. That's what she'd done with the firebirds so long ago, and when she'd first encountered Nox, before approaching him, she'd breached his mind to ensure he wouldn't strike her, a precaution she always took with dangerous things.

"Nekos," he replied. "Felines as tall as you." He smiled, holding his hand up to his pecs to show their height. So, yes, roughly her size. "They're deadly, and they like to play with their food, too. When they take someone down that tunnel, we hear screams for hours."

Nalini winced.

"Some are smaller—the males, we think. No one got close enough to them to check which ones have a pecker."

She looked down the corridor again. "Why are they

in here?" she asked. "Don't they need access to prey? I can't imagine there's much to feed beasts in the mountain. Except the occasional loyalist."

Heio laughed. "Their den is somewhere in these caves, but it leads out."

How *fascinating*. She smiled and purposefully walked away from the tunnel, firmly marking its position in her mind.

This was her way out.

Now she just had to convince Kronos to let her lead him toward a flesh-eating monster's den. Should be a piece of cake.

***

"ARE YOU CERTAIN?"

He couldn't act based on rumors and hearsay; there was a chance he wouldn't act at all, even if the intel Hart reported was, in fact, true.

Kai had fought relentlessly; he now controlled seven of the nine systems of their sector. All of his enemies had allied themselves and conglomerated on the last two. One, Ederia, was inhabited by the civilians who wished to stay away from the worlds he was building, away from magic and from war. Their prerogative. Still, his eyes were on the peaceful system for one reason: he strongly suspected that it was where

Nalini had chosen to hide. It fitted what he knew of her.

The other system, Draks, was the opposite. Its main planet, Nimeria, was the stronghold of the loyalists who wished to restore their previous rule, reinstating slavery and butchering mages. They called it the natural order of things.

Kai stared at the hologram before him, showing both systems.

They were populous, some three billion inhabitants per planet—Evris and other races, too. A fair few Kretians—the blue-skinned, smooth, and short bipeds who rivaled their race in intelligence and surpassed them in cunning. They were merchants by trade and could be found in every system throughout the galaxy.

Kai liked them well enough.

"The Imperials are readying for an attack as we speak, that much is clear. It is my understanding that the emperor has purposefully dispatched his own cousin, and the order wasn't given in a Council session. As a royal, Vuler has the power to take it upon himself to lead a war if he so wishes. That way, the Imperials can pretend to have nothing to do with this."

They were planning to attack Draks. If the Imperials occupied it, they'd have a military base in his sector.

But they'd get rid of Kai's enemies in the process—the loyalists, slavers and barbarians who deserved nothing but death.

Kai wished he could take a knee and think,, but it would have felt awkward in the presence of his cabinet. Instead, he folded his arms behind his back and watched the stars through the large window. Emptying his mind of all concerns, he searched for an answer.

Seconds passed in silence. Kai saw a pair of blue eyes pass through his mind.

Her.

He never felt her these days, although no hour passed without him thinking of her. She'd shut him out, blocking their bond just as he'd become conscious of it.

Yet, he could almost hear her whisper in his ear today.

"There are innocents on Nimeria. Children, Kretians. They'll be slaughtered along with the rest."

The words came out of his mouth, but it was almost as if she were saying them.

"Prepare the fleet. Let us send a message. We will be protecting *our* worlds."

But they were too late.

Nalini felt them before the alarms were raised. She woke with a start and rushed to wake Kronos up; no need, the child had jumped down from his bed and was already tying his boots.

"We need to get out of here. Now."

Something was coming, something big with thousands of souls, all intending destruction. Kai's armies, she supposed. She wouldn't—couldn't—be in the base when they descended upon them, because there was no way in hell she was going to protect the loyalists.

Kronos was ready in minutes; they left all their belongings, just taking the clothes on their backs.

They were halfway through to the tunnels, walking as fast as they could without being obvious in their intention, when a high-pitched siren sounded. In no time, there were soldiers running everywhere, none of whom were paying them any mind, until one rushed to her, calling her name like they were familiar.

Veli Hora. She closed her eyes and counted to ten; by the time he was at her side, her features betrayed nothing more than mild distaste, rather than her desire to crush him with her bare hands.

"Where are you going? There's no time. We've ordered an evacuation," he said, dragging her where he'd just come from. "Let me put you in my transport. It's safest."

She took her hand back and stood her ground. "Yours?" She laughed. "I don't think so."

Veli stilled, watching her closely.

"Look, whatever you've heard, I don't intend to harm you. I never touch ladies. Only slaves."

She hadn't heard a thing about him, but each word coming out of his pretty mouth confirmed the gut feeling she'd had about him from the very start.

"You," he said, "I've never seen a female as precious as you. My intentions are entirely honorable. But now is *not* the time to do this. Just get in a transport and head to safety. This is no simple raid. The *Imperials* are attacking with weapons we can't even identify."

Her eyes widened. After a beat, she took a step back and turned on her heels. "I'll take my chances, thanks."

She heard him make his move, and Nalini smiled. There ended pretense. It didn't matter anyway; she was done with the loyalists' crap, for good.

When he attempted to grab her, she took hold of his arm instead, pulling it to her with all the strength a year fighting with warriors had infused in her small frame. Then she leaped, jumping to his shoulder, breaking his arm. A guttural scream escaped him as she kicked his face, hard, breaking his nose. He fell, unconscious.

He deserved all that and more.

Despite the alarm, everyone in their immediate area had stopped moving, staring wordlessly. She'd not used any magic, not here, and she didn't need it against scum like him. Still, they stared in awe; she was nothing, just an irrelevant healer in gray whom they'd seen running around for a couple of weeks. And she'd taken on one of their highest commanders like he was a weakling.

Nalini spotted Heio amongst the crowd. She didn't mind the foot soldier. Actually, she didn't mind most of the lowly males and females around the base. They didn't seem to have much of an opinion; they just knew Kai had attacked their home, and they'd joined a group that swore to defend it. She hadn't heard demeaning, racist, or sexist comments from them. And then, there were also the slaves. She doubted Veli had arranged transports for them.

"I'll be leaving this hole through the neko den," she informed them. "The beasts won't be a problem. If you don't want to take on the Imperials by air, follow me."

She made one quick detour along the way. Standing in front of the locked doors of three bunkers, Nalini hesitated. She was no hacker. There was only one way to open those doors without a key. Magic.

The doors burst open before she did a thing about it. Turning to her left, she saw Kronos, hand outstretched, his signature yellow energy in hand.

There were terrified whispers behind them. *The boy! The boy is a mage.*

She opened her mouth to ask why he'd done this, but closed it again. She knew why. Kronos was tired of hiding; he'd been tired for a long time now. But she hadn't been ready to expose herself, and he knew it. She'd protected the boy for so long, it was strange to see him return the favor now.

She smiled as the stunned slaves. Some of them had scattered when they'd seen magic. Those who were left would live.

"Let's get out of here."

KRONOS DESTROYED the door at the end of the tunnel; the other side was dark and cold.

"You're sure about this?" Heio asked.

"No," she lied.

There was nothing she feared inside this cave. The only thing she feared was her own race.

"Let's go."

Some stayed back, returning to their stations; a dozen soldiers and all the slaves followed her down the endless maze of tunnels.

They braced themselves, expecting death at each step, but no felines crossed their path; they didn't even go anywhere close to the nekos' den. Heio and the others talked of luck, but Kronos smiled knowingly, seeing Nalini's eyes remaining amber in the darkness.

The felines had been very, very close, but, at her bidding, they remained in the shadows, despite the temptation of their flesh. Oh, how the beasts liked the smell of their flesh. Nalini could almost feel their hunger.

Underneath it all, she felt something else, too.

She turned back toward the caves when they'd reached the other side of the mountain.

It was calling to her, would have said her name if it had known how to speak.

"You look like you're considering something extremely stupid," Kronos said. "Please, tell me I'm wrong."

She rolled her eyes. "Stay with the group, unless they look like they want to burn you at the pyre. I won't be long."

"Unless the Imperials bomb the mountain and you die."

She had to chuckle. "Yes. Unless that."

And, on that note, running, she returned inside the cave, this time turning right when they'd come from the left.

She immediately came face-to-face with one of them. And oh, damn, but Heio had been right. They were huge, bigger than her in fact. The feline's sharp teeth were longer than her entire face. "Good kitty," she said nervously, focusing her mind on it, on keeping it docile.

It took a lot of energy. Animal or not, his mind was strong. "There, there," she said. "Stay put, and don't eat the Nalini."

The neko's head followed her progression, hissing.

As she walked through the tunnels, more of them came to her, each of them challenging her, pushing through her mind. She was sweating by the time the tunnel spilled inside a cavernous, dimly lit cave. Looking up, she found thousands of starbugs on the natural ceiling, each of them adding a little brightness. They really did look like stars in the sky.

There was a shallow fountain at one end of the vast cave, and, next to it, lay the most ginormous of these beasts—so large Nalini doubted she'd fit through any of the tunnels.

She didn't need to pass through, though. No, this beast was fed where she lay. She just looked at any of the others, and they obeyed wordlessly.

This was their queen.

She could have fought Nalini and eaten her then and there, had she wanted to. Instead, she watched her.

Nalini moved toward the ground slowly. One of her knees touched the floor, and then she sat, legs crossed, far from the beast, but it could have, would have, closed the distance in one leap had it wanted to.

"Have you called to trap me here?" she asked, her head tilted.

She should be afraid. She wasn't.

The beast moved, shifting to get to her feet. As she did, Nalini saw the four creatures at her sides. Each of them was huge already over half the size of Nox, although they'd only been born a few days ago.

Her heirs. Two little princes and two princesses.

Three of the felines were already fighting, their little claws outstretched, toothless jaws closing on their siblings' ears and paws. They ignored the last one. Pale and unmoving. Red blood down his leg. Practically dead.

If he stayed on their cold, harsh world, he would die.

Nalini understood then. It hadn't been her power at all that had gotten them through the tunnels. How arrogant she was, believing herself strong enough to subdue all the beasts, just because they had fur and claws.

She, Kronos, and the others had been allowed safe passage by the queen of these tunnels for one simple reason.

Nalini crawled forward slowly, taking care not to touch the three children that weren't hers to care for.

"He'll be safe with me," she promised, gathering the weak body in her arms, noticing his shallow breaths.

The queen didn't talk, but she might as well have.

He better be.

Nalini got out of there before the neko queen changed her mind She was still in the tunnels when an explosion took down half the mountain. She *felt* it. It should have destroyed everything; there was no logical reason why these tunnels were holding above her head.

Only magic could have done that.

She stole one last glance backward. Amber eyes, not unlike hers, watched her in the darkness.

Nalini hastened, clutching the neko closer against her heart. She emerged out of the mountain a little more knowledgeable about the world.

The skies above the mountain were clouded, stars hidden by two humongous ships that turned their day to night. One of the ships, and all its fleet, were retreating; it fled, jumping to warp. Hopefully, that was good news.

Tracking Kronos's familiar mind signature, she found her group with ease. They'd arrived at a clearing, and all of them stood, hands held up in surrender. Two dozen soldiers in exosuits held them at gunpoint.

She froze. She stopped moving, thinking, breathing.

The soldiers didn't retain her attention.

There, in the darkened clearing, an immaculate cloak over his combat gear, a white and red mask over his head, stood Kai Lor Hora.

He didn't know how he managed to keep it in check, but he forced himself to remain where he stood.

Nalini. He felt her. Smelled her. He had to hold on to what remained of his senses as everything in him stopped and then started again, recalibrated, reborn.

Finally, he turned to her. He'd purposefully avoided looking at her until then, needing an instant to prepare himself for it.

She was it now. Completely. His dreams and nightmares, the vision he couldn't chase away. Sometime over the last few years, she'd completed the tattoo around the scar that ran along her shoulder and down her arm. Right now, as he looked at her, both of her eyes were blue, like they'd been in the vision branded in his memory so long ago.

She was dressed plainly, in dark gray, cheap cloth, not the colorful satins, velvets, and leather he would shower upon her. Seeing him, the female froze, her eyes widening in surprise and concern.

Kai noticed him then. The male who rushed next to her, adopting a possessive, protective stance. His veins turned to ice. Looking away from her took every bit of self-control he'd gained over the course of the three decades he'd lived through.

But somehow, he managed.

He signaled the leader of a small unit. "Take them to the Dominion," he ordered sternly. "Give them private quarters."

His order would have been different if Nalini hadn't been amongst them. Eight amongst the group wore loyalist colors. They were prisoners, at best.

"Yes, sir."

"Everyone else, with me."

And he advanced, heading out to secure the rest of the planet.

What was left of it, in any case.

He'd only moved three steps when he heard her voice.

"Just try to touch me, see how it turns out for you."

Kai smiled. A tigress. She was a tigress. He saw it in her fierce eyes, in the way she held herself. Five foot six, tops, when most females reached five ten. Males topped her at six foot three or more. Yet turning to see what it had all been about, he saw the squad leader squirm.

The male bravely stood his ground. "The beast can't come. Might be infested. We have strict directives aboard the Dominion to keep the environment clean and safe for everyone."

"Then fucking leave me here," she countered.

Kai turned on his heels and advanced toward her, each of his steps purposeful. He would have been logical and reasonable about this, had she not said those precise words.

Leave her here? He glowered.

Kai stood right in front of her and stared. Even Ian Krane would have faltered under *that* look. She stared back defiantly.

"I'm not going anywhere without this neko," she informed him.

Kai glanced down toward the animal in her arms. A young, wild beast, dirty and sick.

"No, I don't suppose I can stop you from saving a pathetic creature at your mercy."

He found himself smiling.

"We have a veterinarian on board. The beast will be cared for." So would she. He didn't add that. "I'm in charge of this evacuation. You're going onto my ship. Tell me we understand each other, Nalini Nova."

«Tell me you'll be in the Dominion when I head back.»

He didn't say those words out loud, but she'd heard them, he was certain of that. Yet, she gave no answer.

Which left him no choice.

Kai turned to the squad leader. "You're now in charge. See that this operation goes according to plan."

He wasn't losing her again. He just wasn't.

He'd found her. Finally, after all this time, he'd found her. She was really here, not a vision based stars away. He felt her mind. Smelled her. Apple, cinnamon, pine, and Heaven all wrapped in one heady flagrance. A scent that could drive him mad, engulfed his senses.

She was small, yet not fragile. The voice, the gaze, the presence—it was all strength. She had an inherently majestic way of moving and talking.

She was a queen. His queen.

Now, it was just a matter of holding on to her.

«*Come with me, Nalini. We'll talk... later. And I'll let you go if you demand it of me.*»

He gestured her forward, and remained in that position until she sighed.

"Alright. Show the way."

Glaring all the way, she nonetheless moved, following him as he walked toward his ship. He felt the corner of his lips inch up under his mask.

Finally. Fucking finally.

WE'LL TALK... later.

The words were a haunting promise.

They ran through Nalini's mind, again and again, as she followed silently, her eyes never leaving his back. Their transport left the ground, heading up towards a sleek, black, gorgeous, custom command ship. Only the best for the warlord, she supposed.

They reached it in no time, speeding through clearance when Kai talked to the command ship's security guy, simply stating, "It's me."

The shields were lowered immediately without anyone asking for a code.

The transport's doors slid open, and Kronos gasped as

his eyes took in the seemingly endless white hall, where thousands of such transports were neatly parked. Nalini just glanced at her new surroundings before her gaze returned to the warlord.

It was really him under the mask. Kai. The subject of her every dream and nightmare. The main character in most of her visions. Darkness reborn.

He was cold. He gave orders that sounded like threats; his enforcers tripped on their own feet to obey rather than face the consequences.

And yet....

Kai was the first to step out of the transport; he was greeted by half a dozen enforcers ready to take his orders.

Kronos leaped out after him.

Nalini's hands were filled by the sleeping neko, or she would have held him back—by his arm, hair, or the scruff of his neck if necessary—as he smiled and dashed up front, passing through three rows of enforcers.

He stood next to Kai's imposing figure.

Nalini groaned.

"Hey, I recognize the presence," the boy announced. "Wanted to say thank you for last time, for... you know."

Oh. Bringing him back to life. Of course, he wanted to thank him for that.

"You've already expressed your thanks. It wasn't required the first time around."

Cold. So cold and formal, even with an enthusiastic teenager.

"All the same," Kronos insisted, not bothered by Kai's response. "I figured we wouldn't see much of you after this, so I wanted to say it while I got the chance."

Kai stopped, looking right at the boy through his visor. The twelve enforcers behind him had come to a halt. He gestured two men forward wordlessly.

"The boy and his caretaker," he said, rather than pronouncing her name; again, acting like he didn't know her. Nalini knew it wouldn't last. "Take them to Clera before assigning them a residence in the upper deck."

"Yes, sir."

He went back on his way, cape floating behind him, not sparing her a glance.

Her heart rate slowly returned to a more appropriate rhythm.

"This way," one enforcer indicated, pointing to the opposite way from the direction Kai had just gone.

"Where are we heading?"

"To Clera, ma'am. The veterinarian on board."

An unexpected rush of grateful surprise seized her. Kai had prioritized the neko's health to whatever showdown he'd planned between them, which was not what she'd expected at all.

The vet was stationed at the forefront of the medical bay, in an elegant office with translucent walls. She welcomed them with open arms and a ready smile.

"I haven't gotten to treat a feline in a long time." She seemed enthusiastic at the thought. "And never one of *these*. Is it truly a nekoderian? I don't think anyone I know is crazy enough to get close to their den."

"I can't say I know much about the race at all," Nalini admitted.

The vet's careful hands found the neko's neck and spiked it with a tranquilizer before she started to work on his wound, cleaning it and then sealing it with a machine that neatly sewed him up in an instant. As she worked, she talked, bringing Nalini up to speed.

"This's one of the old races our ancients revered back on Tejen; so they brought some with them once they started exploring space. The same way our people used to bond with dragons, some mages formed a bond with these creatures. But then mages were slaughtered, and the nekos' descendants were born in the wild. There's a few of them on most planets in the Belt, less in the Empire. You're fortunate to have found one so young; but, regardless, once he heals, you'll have to let him go back to the wild." She smiled sadly, not unkindly. "Only mages can hope to control these beasts."

The female was assuming that she was a regular. Nalini smiled. "I just want him to get better."

The stars knew, if he didn't, his mother would hunt her down and kill her—slowly.

"Great. Well, I'm done here. He'll be grumpy when he wakes up, and I want to check his vitals. Leave him with me. I'll comm you when he's ready to be picked up."

Nalini frowned. "I don't have any comm device on me."

Clera smiled kindly. "You'll get one on debriefing. Search for me and dump your ID number in my messages."

The enforcers led them out of the medical bay. As they did, Nalini had to point out, "Your orders were to take us to our residence, not to debriefing."

Under their exosuits, the men were so nervous, they sweated. Probing a little deeper, Nalini felt their anxiety. Nothing had gone according to plan since they'd landed on Nimeria. Kai had gone off script. And he never did. That confused and frightened the daylights out of both of them.

The male on the right, Park, was Kai's best guard. On the left, Ollis was the second best. That both of them had been dispatched to take care of her shocked them, and they took this job seriously. Very, very seriously.

Nalini wanted to tell them to chill out. She simply was a valuable asset Kai didn't mean to lose. Enlil had also set his best troops on her.

"Yes, ma'am," Park replied formally. "We're taking you up to your quarters right now."

Another detail that made them uncomfortable: *everyone* went through debrief, not just newcomers. Even Kai had his own debrief meeting with his cabinet after every mission. The very first meeting strangers passed was crucial; it determined who was a potential spy, for one.

She and Kronos were spared the hour-long ordeal, although they'd been with *loyalists*. Park and Ollis were sweating. The whole thing stressed them out.

Again, she wanted to pat the males on their shoulders and tell them to chill. Kai was simply planning to make her squirm in a meeting himself.

They took her to the upper deck, where officers were

stationed. Ollis and Park's own places weren't far. Each apartment had large rooms, equipped with entertainment and little kitchens, lounges, and individual showers. Below, the rooms were only slightly larger than broom closets, and the common folk had to deal with communal bathrooms.

Nalini shuddered and blessed her stars. *Communal bathrooms.* She would have jumped in the void of space without a suit within one week, tops.

They never commented upon it, professional to a tee.

"You'll find the apartment fully functional. Should you wish for anything, a domestic android will be at your service. If that fails, you can call to maintenance or housekeeping through the comm situated next to the door," Park said, opening their door.

Both enforcers froze right there.

When they entered the dark room, she felt him immediately; only Kronos displayed any surprised when he turned the lights on to find Kai standing next to their main window, arms crossed behind his back, looking at the skies.

TWENTY-SIX

BEHIND THE MASK

"I s there anywhere Kronos can hang out?" she asked the stunned guards still behind her.

They hesitated for half a beat.

"Yeah. Yeah, sure. We'll take him down to training. My lord?" Ollis checked it was all right.

Kai finally turned.

He'd removed the mask and the pieces of armor, yet it felt like he was even more imposing now.

"Thank you, Ollis."

The enforcers practically ran out of there, urging the boy to follow.

"You terrorize them," was the first thing Nalini said.

Kai's dark eyes set on hers, and a slow smile spread on his face.

"Actually, both Park and Ollis are friends of mine. You'll find that it's you they aren't sure about."

He paced like a wolf, deliberately slow, walking in circles, occupying the entire space.

Nalini sat on an ergonomic chair next to a mini bar. Hiding her anxiety as best she could, she investigated the contents of the cold compartments. She wasn't much for spirits, but well, it had been one of those days.

"Drink?" she offered.

"I don't drink."

"Not even today?" she asked. Then she laughed; how silly of her. Today might fuck with her mind and her nerves, but it was just another day for him, no doubt. "Well, more for me."

She poured herself a couple of fingers of a clear, sweet liqueur. Kai observed her every motion before closing the distance between them, coming to stand right next to where she'd sat.

Breathe, she admonished herself, in vain.

His fingers brushed hers as he seized the glass she'd just poured.

"Very wise of you."

He took the glass and moved to sit on the armchair

right in front of her as she poured herself another one.

Even then, his imposing stature dwarfed hers.

"Hardly."

Watching him was too unsettling, so she looked around. The spaceship's cabins had been designed to look homey; this one, in any case.

"Not what I expected," she admitted.

"No, I'd wager not. You thought I'd cage you. Bind your wrists. Torture you, no doubt. Keep you locked in a barren room and hit you when I cared to."

She shrugged unapologetically. "You might have learned by now. If you go prying through people's minds, you might not like what you see."

He lifted a brow. "I'm not trying, Nalini. You broadcast your every thought." That teasing smile flashed again. "I would have expected so proficient a psychic to be better at keeping her shields up."

She rolled her eyes.

"Sixteen years," he mused, "since we were last in the same room. Fourteen since you saved my life for the second time. And two since one of my men killed your child."

She looked away. Even just thinking of that day still felt like plunging a sword through her beating heart.

"It's been a long time." He downed his drink in one go. "Tell me."

Nalini frowned. "What?"

"Everything."

Those eyes. That look. She couldn't take it, and couldn't look away, either. If she hadn't known better, she would have thought he was sending some compulsion to bend her to his will, but she would have felt it. This was no order. He was... asking her to share her life. Why, she didn't know.

"I watched it all," he said. "My men made a short cut through your life to give me an idea, but I pulled all the recordings and fast-forwarded through them. Sometimes, when I have time, I pull some of them out. I watch you getting shocked in your cage. Then I remember why I'm doing this. I've seen it, I don't need information. But tell me what it was like for you, back then. What you've done with your life since. You went off radar. How? What was that place I saw last year? Tell me."

He made it sound like he was simply curious about her. She knew better than to think that was all. He was a warlord. He wanted—

"Stop assuming." An order. He softened it, by adding, "Everything you guess about my intentions is entirely erroneous. Look for answers if you must."

Was he truly inviting her into his mind?

"Yes. Yes, I am, Nalini."

"Will you *stop* reading my mind? Ever heard of the word private?"

This time, his smile showed white, white teeth. "I told you. I'm not looking. You're broadcasting."

She wasn't. Right?

"Go on, look." His words were a caress. "I dare you."

That was unfair, and showed how well he understood her. He shouldn't have; as he'd pointed out, they'd met less than a handful of times. But already, he knew she couldn't resist bets.

Sighing, and bracing herself for the upcoming battle, she concentrated on him, both her eyes gold. They returned to blue almost immediately, finding his shields down. Open.

Her hand, that had instinctively moved to reach toward him, lowered, dropping at her side.

His mind was peaceful. Quiet.

Loving.

He thought of nothing else than caring for others. He'd been right. Nothing she saw computed with her vision of him.

Traveling through his thoughts, she saw him looking

for her through time, searching, always keeping his ear on the ground about her location. And she saw his goal. His intention.

Protecting her, the child he owed everything to. She'd earned peace. She'd earned safety.

Then, there was that day, the day when he finally found information about her. Seen the recordings, and realized—

She hit a wall for the first time.

He was done sharing.

Nalini almost protested, tried to hit against the wall, but she stopped herself. Already, she'd pried more than she was entitled to—if anyone was entitled to a glimpse through someone else's mind at all.

"I'm not the monster you think I am," he said softly.

He really, really wasn't.

Feeling the need to justify herself, she stated, "I saw that you were Darkness. And you can mold Starfire, Kai. I..." She stopped, realizing she was making a bigger mess of things. "I'm sorry. You're no monster at all. I just saw so many visions of destruction."

"Oh, I am a monster, little lady. Just not one you should fear."

He got up and made them a second drink.

"You saw me bring ruin and fire. To protect those who can't fight for themselves, I have, for years now. Wars aren't pretty."

She accepted the drink he handed her. He then remained standing and started slowly pacing again.

"You talk of your visions. Have you ever seen my wife?" he asked. "My children?"

Nalini was shocked. She shouldn't have been; back in the day, whenever a guard had managed to get her alone for a minute, they would ask the very same question. Would they be married someday, have sons or daughters? But it didn't seem like the sort of concern she would have anticipated, coming from him.

She shook her head. "Sorry, no. It doesn't mean you never find anyone; I don't see everything."

Kai laughed. "Of course you don't."

She could have offered to look for him. Give him answers if she could find them. She remained silent.

Back at the spot where he'd been when she'd entered the room, in front of the window, he asked again, "Tell me. I'd like to get to know you."

Nalini bit her lip. Her life hadn't been pretty at first, and then it became boring before taking a turn for the weird. She'd never spoken of it. Why would she? There was no one she trusted, save for Krane and

Kronos, and the kid had followed her every step along the way since they met. As for Krane, the old male had seemed to know most things about her; and if there was anything he didn't know, he hadn't bothered to ask.

But she talked; she owed him that much. And, wordlessly, with a rapt attention, never interrupting her, he listened.

Finally, she was done. After a long silence, Kai laughed. "Krane is a Wise. I should have known."

She would have thought that he'd ask after his brother first, expecting either hatred or curiosity about him, but on that subject he remained silent. She got it. She wouldn't have had much to ask about her family, either.

She had to point out, "I realized that right away."

"Yeah, well, not all of us are seers. Besides, I met him when I was very young." He added, "Glad to know Nox is well."

"You know his wolf?"

Kai nodded slowly. "Left Haimo with me a long, long time ago."

This time, it was her turn to ask, "Tell me?"

And to her surprise, he ran through the thirty-five

years of his life, baring them to her with little to no filter, gruesome details and all. Unapologetic. True.

She wondered how long they'd been talking by the time he stiffened, touching the comm device fitted along his jaw. "Got it. I'll be on the bridge shortly."

"Sorry for keeping you. I guess you have a lot to do. Worlds to run and all that."

How laughable it was to her, when she didn't always remember to pay her comm bill on time.

Kai remained in his place of choice for a few moments. "I keep my word. Should you wish to, we'll drop you off in a safe system. But you have a place here." She made no immediate answer, and he didn't seem to expect her to. "You'll have clearance on all levels. I'll get someone to take your fingerprints later, to let you access restricted areas. And they'll drop a comm. Go as you please."

On that note, the warlord retrieved the mask he'd left on an empty shelf and left her apartment.

She took a long, hot shower, running through the latest developments in her crazy life, half wishing she hadn't been such a coward and run to him as she'd longed to at seventeen, half knowing everything had occurred exactly as it should have.

S he woke up early again. Finding the space that the neko had claimed at the foot of her bed empty and cold, she frowned. Rather than attempting to catch a few more hours of sleep, she dragged her ass out of bed and slowly pulled her gray slacks up her limbs in silence to avoid waking Kronos up.

The silly feline could get into some trouble. And if he felt threatened, he could hurt himself again trying to get away. Kai had allowed him to be brought on board because she'd pouted and made a little scene right in front of everyone; he was her responsibility now, even though the adorable creature was potentially an evil fiend in disguise.

Nalini knew what his presence felt like; tracking it through the maze of high- tech, lit -up corridors wasn't hard. She tensed as her steps inexorably took her to the front of the ship on the highest level. No. Surely not even he was that freaking evil, right?

But indeed. Nalini drew her breath, standing right in front of the large, tall doors that couldn't be mistaken as anything but the command platform of the vessel. The neko was right through these doors, she knew it.

She remained planted on her feet, horrified and frozen. What now?

Before she could make up her mind, the two large doors parted. Five Evris stared at her from the platform. A beautiful female in a small pink top and a tight suit that didn't cover much of her athletic frame; a large, goofy, smiling male her age; two elegantly dressed people who looked very much alike, although one of them was male and the other female; and him. Kai Lor of Hora. An impossibly tall wolf at his side, bigger than Nox.

And Kai had the damn neko in his arms.

He faced away from her, observing space through a large panoramic screen. Windows were apparently his thing.

"Come on in, Nalini," he said, without so much as turning her way. "Unless you'd like one of those regular, loyalist friends of yours to find you here."

She stayed put another second, finding it impossible to move; then his words sank in.

Shit. What if she *was* found here in the early hours of the morning?

Her simple life down on one of these planets they passed by depended on her discretion. If anyone learned that she was a mage, or simply that she was associated with Kai at all, that would be it.

She rushed forward, entering the command bridge. The doors closed behind her, and only then did Kai turn. He took her breath away again; her memory never did him justice. He truly was the most painfully striking male she'd ever seen.

Even when his arm was getting savagely scratched by a neko kitten. Nalini couldn't help a chuckle.

"Funny, is it?" he challenged, glaring. "This beast stormed in here, terrorized Sky, and tricked me into pulling him away. Now he's attached himself to my arm, only to bite, draw blood, and spit at me. Many have been destroyed for less."

The four people in the room had a hard time containing their laughter.

"Evi," the female in pink introduced herself, holding her hand out. Nalini went to shake it. "I'm the general of the fleet. This is Wench, our engineer in chief, and the twins—Star and Hart. They're both Coats." Nalini's confusion must have been visible, because Evi clarified, "Politicians. They belong to opposite parties."

Indeed, Hart was clad in a long black and green robe that connoted a naturalist affiliation, while Star wore black and blue. She was with the technologists.

One of Nalini's brows lifted. "I can only imagine the family dinners."

Nats and Techs were always bickering about one thing or another.

The Coats laughed. "You have no idea," Star replied. "Our mother is an Imperial, and our father, a loyalist at heart. If we all have to be in the same room, no subject is safe, not even the weather."

She winced on their behalf, before waving around the room to everyone.

"Nice to meet you all," she replied awkwardly. "Nalini."

Wench smiled in response. "We know."

Oh. They'd heard of her, from Kai that meant. She bit her lip, wondering what he'd said about her. Rather than ask that, she held her hand up while walking toward the silent warlord, who observed her with his keen, intense eyes, making her uncomfortable as ever.

"I'll take him, and try to keep him in the residential levels."

And she tried, but the neko started to scratch frantically, before wrapping his paws around Kai's arm, making it quite clear he intended to stay where he was. His hind legs tapped against Kai's sleeve frantically, and he turned on his back, sending a pleading look with his big round eyes.

Kai grimaced, all the while giving in, stroking the beast with his free hand. "He does that routine as soon as I move to put him down. I swear that thing can get away with anything."

"He's a demon," Nalini nodded. "Sorry."

Kai shrugged like it didn't matter at all. Then, as though there was no intruder in his high command, he talked, no doubt carrying on the conversation they'd been having before her arrival.

"It's going to be a risky move. I don't want to order anyone to go to their doom. We'll call for volunteers only."

"I'll go," the pink-clad general announced. "We need a description of their weapon. All we heard is that it destroyed half the city with one blast. Having details could save so many lives."

Nalini felt like she should have made herself scarce at first, but she paused. They were talking about the Imperial attack on the Nimerian base, she realized.

"Not you," Kai shook his head. "You're too valuable."

The way he said it made Nalini look at Evi again. She

really was very beautiful, almost as much as him. She made sense for him; they were a remarkable pair, Nalini noted.

And that second, she hated the other female for it. *Hated* her. Pure, undiluted jealousy poisoned her heart.

Kai turned to her, frowning, watching her too closely. Shit. His damn ability to read her thoughts, despite her shields, despite the fact that he wasn't trying. She forced herself to pull more shields between them, until she couldn't feel him at all. It took a lot of effort, like her mind revolted against protecting itself from him. Which was weird and ridiculous.

"I should go. I'll come back later for—"

"You were in Nimeria during the attack," Kai stated. "Can you concur? Was it truly one blast?"

Nalini stilled before nodding. "Yes. I was out of range, but I felt it. The ground trembled. Something blinding flashed; I had to close my eyes. Everyone...." Her voice lowered to a whisper and faded.

She wasn't going to say the rest of what happened, when it would have clued anyone in on what she was.

"You can talk. Everyone in this room already knows you're one of us, Nalini."

Her head snapped up.

"They know how you saved me." To his men, he explained, "Nalini works as a healer or a cargo pilot for whoever pays her well enough. Of late, it was the loyalists on Nimeria."

He said it without judgement, but one of his men laughed, making her feel inadequate. That he'd shared what she'd told him privately made her blood boil. It was a challenge, and she could have replied any manner of ways.

No one expected her to move to slap the warlord of their entire sector.

Kai stopped her hand before she'd landed a hit. Then a slow, leisurely smile formed on his lips. A truly terrifying smile, cruel and wicked.

She shivered, her eyes widening at her own actions.

What was she thinking? The male could have her whipped for that. Or locked in a cage and shocked.

"Feisty still, I see," he said, releasing her hand.

"You don't get to judge me. You don't know a thing about me."

He lifted a brow before turning away from her.

She was dismissed.

"You can't go, Evi. I need you up here, keeping things together. What we need is spies, not forces. Simple, inconspicuous individuals who can blend in and keep their head while on the ground. We'll ask for volunteers, put together a team in the morning. Now, give me some good news."

Nalini started to move toward the doors. She'd taken three steps when Kai called her back.

"Nalini?"

She stilled, but didn't turn.

«*I didn't mean to offend. Don't leave angry.*»

Out loud, he just said, "Keep your comm on. I'll let you know when this beast of yours is more amenable."

The doors in front of her remained closed. She sighed.

«*It's fine. I'm just a little touchy.*»

The doors opened.

Damn pushy, psychic warlord.

The neko appeared at dinnertime and deigned to stay long enough to get a few scratches on top of his head, neck, and back, while he digested. When she awoke again the next day, he was gone. She didn't make the mistake of hunting him down a second time.

An instructor came to take Kronos for school; then, after catching some breakfast, Nalini went to explore. She'd been given complete clearance, as promised.

The lower levels of the ship were vast, so vast the ship could have comfortably housed twice as many people as it currently did, although she knew there had been thousands of enforcers and as many Nimerians.

Hours into her little tour, after stumbling upon a park with real plants, a pond, and some nice holographic views, as well as a financial center, a library, and a gym, she realized that their humongous eyesore of a ship was nothing short of a city in the skies.

She wandered aimlessly, all the while wondering how long their welcome would last. These people, everyone of age, seemed to have a purpose, but Nalini and the Nimerians were just there, without having much to do, taking up their resources. Kai hadn't seemed to want to kick her out, but still. He certainly didn't intend to let her stay indefinitely.

What would her next step be, now? Where would she and Kronos go?

Normally, the answer to that question came naturally. She just had to think about the place where her enemies were least likely to look for her. But what enemy? Now she was certain Kai didn't mean her harm, she realized she had none. She was safe. She could – they could – in fact, stay here, if there was a place for her. Some sort of job she could take.

Nalini had let her thoughts wander and walked aimlessly for a long time. She suddenly realized how far her steps had taken her. The corridors were different here. Larger, lighter, a little less plain and white. There was a thin, barely noticeable gold line along each wall at eye level. She stopped too late.

A door opened in front of a half-naked Kai, breathing hard, glistening with sweat. Her mouth popped open in shock, and she stared, wordlessly. Could anyone so perfect be real? Actually real? Each part of his body seemed to have been sculpted with care, molded into a hard, golden statue. Nalini found it hard to breathe. Her tongue darted out to wet her bottom lip, and, realizing what she'd just done, she bit it back in. Oh god, someone kill her before she started drooling.

Kai stopped as soon as he saw her. He seemed both surprised and confused at finding her there. Not displeased, though.

The door opened again, and Evi emerged, chuckling. "Wait, come back!" she called to Kai. "It's not nearly as much fun without you."

Oh. She'd interrupted something. Shit. Shit.

"Sorry, I—wrong turn," she mumbled.

Damn her stupid, stupid feet for leading her there. She moved to leave, but a hand took her wrist and pulled her forward.

"Oh no, you don't. You've made it just in time. Trust me on this, you don't want to miss this," Evi said, laughing as she dragged Nalini through the doors she'd just come out of.

Nalini's protests died on her lips when she found a gym inside. Relief flooded her. They hadn't been getting sweaty in the way she'd imagined then. Not that it mattered. It *didn't,* she insistently told herself.

If they'd been occupied fucking like bunnies in a kinky antigravity room, it would have been none of her business, dammit.

Turned out, Evi was right; she really, really didn't want to miss what was happening in there.

In the large room, there were various machines, currently neglected as every person present stood in circle around a ring.

Two very well-defined males were sparring—a ruthless, brutal fight that didn't seem to have any defined rules. They practically tore each other apart as a small crowd cheered for their respective champion. Lesser fighters would truly have killed each other using that kind of strength, but they knew what they were doing. Vicious and willing to hurt, they avoided all vital areas and never took things too far.

Nalini watched them eagerly, enjoying the display of strength and skills. She picked a favorite and cheered along with the rest of them, until he won.

"This is awesome! No magic, right?"

She'd asked Evi, but Kai responded from behind her. She'd felt him reenter the gym with them.

"That's it. There's a few fights once a week or so. We have to stay in good physical form; otherwise our powers run out quicker, as you'd know."

She did know this. Ian Krane had ingrained it into

her mind; and, as usual, the old male wasn't wrong. She'd grown much stronger since she'd learned to push herself. More settled, too. Perhaps even happier.

She smiled. "It looks like fun."

There was a snort from behind her.

That got her attention. Nalini turned, one eyebrow lifted.

"Oh?"

"I have a hard time imagining you in there." The infuriating male shrugged unapologetically. "Nothing sexist; Evi and a bunch of females in our rank hold their own, against males, too, but you aren't really built for this."

She glared.

"Well, it might be hard, as I don't think anyone would throw the fight to let *me* win, like they might for their warlord."

Evi took an intake of breath, and Kai just stared at her before laughing. Downright laughing in her face.

"Yeah, sure. Cute, *little* lady." The dick insisted on the term *little*.

She shrugged. "All I'm saying is, I can't imagine anyone gives 100 percent when they fight against their lord and master."

"I'm no one's master," he retorted, his infuriating gaze settling on her. That grin that unsettled her flashed again. "All right, I'll bite. You, me, in there. If you can hold on against me without begging me to stop for, let's say, five minutes, I'll bow to you and apologize for underestimating you."

She noticed the crowd had stopped paying any mind to the previous fighters, and they were now focused on them. He held his hand out, and she moved to shake it when he added, "And when you lose, you'll bow to *me*."

Nalini stopped. Bowing. She hadn't bowed since she was seventeen. To another warlord. One who expected it.

"I won't think less of you for backing out, Nalini," the infuriating male taunted.

So she closed the distance between them and shook his damn hand.

"There's that spunk. Don't worry, little lady, I won't go too hard on you."

Of all the egotistical things he could have said.

Nalini scanned the faces around, suddenly panicked. Kai caught her hesitation. "All right everyone, whatever the outcome, this stays within these walls."

They all agreed, and they *wouldn't* betray Kai, she knew that. So she moved to the ring, removing her jacket. Half a dozen mages hooted encouragingly, while another twenty laughed, no doubt thinking her insane for even attempting to stand against the mountain of pure taut muscle.

Kai entered the ring before her. He'd already fought, or at least exerted himself on one of these machines today, or he wouldn't have gotten quite so sweaty. She could use that to her advantage.

"All right, I'll ref," a guy volunteered. "No magic. No deadly blows."

Evi whistled to get Nalini's attention. "Hey girl, betting a fifty on ya. Better not let me down." She winked, making Nalini laugh. "Five minutes. You got this."

She did.

Nalini parted her legs and bent down, reaching her toes, stretching her neck. It had been a while since she'd had a chance to train. She found her stupid cargo pants tight and just decided to remove them, as she wore black boy shorts underneath. Nothing more outrageous than Evi's clothing.

Some guys laughed and hooted.

Kai stated, "That's cheating. She's obviously trying to distract me."

She saw the ref shrug. "Not against the rules."

Kai sighed. "Fine. I'll win either way."

"Ten seconds. Nine. Eight."

She kept stretching until the ref was down to two. Then, she walked to the middle of the ring, facing Kai, who watched her like prey, eyes twinkling dangerously.

She sent him a smile of her own when the ref finally said, "Go!"

He was bigger, taller, and definitely stronger than her. Five minutes. This was, or should have been, a game of endurance and skills. But what was the fun in that? She didn't want to last five minutes; she wanted to put him on his ass and shut him up.

So, she did just that. Nalini attacked, jumping to his neck and flipping him to the mat; she beamed, towering over him, one knee on his chest. She knew she'd only managed because he was stunned, shocked.

"If we were in battle, you'd be dead by now."

Then, from underneath her, Kai laughed and simply got up, carrying her like she weighed nothing. She probably did to him. With one arm, he held her against his impossibly hard frame as he tried to get hold of her arm with his free hand. She freed herself before he could, kicking him in the nuts to get away.

Kai winced and groaned, taking the hit without crying, but only just.

Then, he lunged himself at her, not holding back. She laughed nervously and attacked furiously. Defense against a male like this was nothing short of suicidal. He was trying to restrain her at first, force her submission, rather than really fight her, but once he realized he couldn't, he let go of restraint. She just avoided a punch that might have knocked her out, responding with a roundhouse kick he blocked. In no time, she was sweating, panting, fighting against this force of nature. Nalini's heart had never worked that hard, her throat was dry, and soon—too soon—everything hurt. Weren't five minutes gone already?

Finally, *finally,* she saw an opening and took it, grabbing his fist and locking his arm behind his back, just like he'd tried to do to her.

She didn't think she'd ever breathed that hard, and it was very possible that she might spit out her lungs any minute, but she had him. He knew it. She knew it. But she was petty enough to want to hear him say it too.

"Do you yield?"

The room was utterly silent.

"Never."

She tightened her hold, making him wince. Kai

laughed and simply turned around. She heard his bone break and winced on his behalf. She was too stunned by his action to think of stopping him from turning the tables. Kai kicked her onto the ground, flipped her over, dropped his weight, and locked her arm. As she had no intention of breaking hers, he'd won.

After a beat, he got up and offered his unbroken arm to help her up. She took it, still stunned and confused. They were just sparring, but he'd *broken his own arm* to win. Shaking her head, she told him, "You're insane," while taking his arm and setting the bone back into place.

He barely winced. She wondered how many times he'd broken bones. Mages healed much faster than regular Evris; they could manipulate energy to speed up the process. It would be good as new by morning, but it was going to hurt like hell.

"Stupid, stupid male." She had to laugh.

"I don't believe any argument against that statement would seem quite valid right now," he admitted, wincing. "It kind of hurt."

"Kind of?"

Then, shocking her beyond words, the warlord took a knee and bowed his head.

"Thirteen minutes," the ref announced, a watch in

hand. "Thirteen fucking minutes. I don't think anyone has ever lasted as long against you, Kai."

"Not once," Kai confirmed. Then his said, looking right into her eyes, "I truly am sorry for underestimating you, Nalini Nova. Trust that it won't happen again."

She put her cargo pants and jacket back on, all the while thinking that she wouldn't underestimate him, either. He'd just proved he'd do absolutely anything to win.

TWENTY-NINE
FLESH AND BLOOD

He often dreamt of her. In the past, she'd remained a willowy shadow in the distance, untouchable, like a holy goddess too pure for any Evris, let alone him.

That night, he imagined her legs spread, sitting on the captain's chair of his bridge, as he knelt in front of her, head buried at the apex of her sex. She kept him there, one hand holding him down, as she played with her ample breast with the other hand.

She wasn't an effigy he should protect, admire, and relinquish. She was flesh, blood, and heart. A fierce warrior who could take him. *Him.* His true equal.

He shouldn't have been surprised. Nothing and no one else would have completed him that way.

The day after that dream, things were quite uncomfortable for him. Her evil feline persisted in coming to his bridge, and this time Nalini did follow him. Seeing her so close to the chair where he'd eaten her out all night long—at least in his mind—amused and frustrated him, and made him readjust himself a few times.

Nalini didn't dare sit anywhere when she came here. She simply lingered in the background, attempting, and failing, to remain unnoticed, until her neko consented to leave Kai's arms. Then, she carried him down to his daily appointment at the vet.

Today, Kai just couldn't bear it.

"Nalini."

She lifted her eyes to where he stood on the command platform, in front of a holographic map of the sector marked with strategic notes.

Kai pointed to a familiar area. "You've lived in Itri. What do you think?" he asked.

She tiptoed until she came around the table, between Evi and Hart.

At her place. At long last.

Close to it, in any case.

"What am I looking at?"

Star clued her in. "The most vulnerable systems in our sector. We're sending additional troops where we can. We can spare one command ship with five hundred light fighters, either going to the Var or Krazu."

She bit her lip. "Don't ask me, I'm biased. Against Itri," she clarified.

Kai wanted to know why. He wanted to know *everything* about this female.

But he'd frightened her away once already with his forcefulness. Let her come to him now. Let her share parts of her because she wanted to.

And, at the end of the day, it mattered little. They could have flipped a coin about the direction of the handful of battalions.

"Krazu, then," he settled. "Make the preparations."

Evi nodded and moved to her station to get the ship dispatched immediately.

He changed the subject, attacking the next item on his very, very long to- do list, all the while noticing the way Nalini looked at him, inquisitively, like she was attempting to make him out.

Strange. He hadn't believed himself capable of feeling quite so self-conscious.

"Any news on that weapon?" he asked around.

"Not yet," Evi replied without ceasing to type directives on her command platform. "The spies are in place, but they just got there. They know how important it is, though."

He hadn't expected much yet. Next, he turned to Hart and Star.

"Other news?"

They always had something to say.

"There's a festival of lights being held on Vratis. The people hope that you may attend. Given the circumstances, I gave no response, but it would be good for morale if you did attend. It's your principal system, and you've barely showed your face there."

"I went three times over the last year," Kai protested.

"Yes, but the previous warlord actually lived there. Barely ever left. They get that things are changing, but remember – most Coats, the Merchant Guild – *everyone* of importance is based there. You need to kiss babies."

Kai sighed. Posturing was getting old incredible quick.

"I remember those nights. I could hear it from my windows. Everyone below danced and laughed. I could... feel their happiness. It was one of the good nights." Nalini said it with a delighted smile, like she was sharing a happy memory, not a nightmare.

Wench looked like he'd seen a ghost. Kai felt like

someone was twisting a knife in his entrails. They both remembered too well their glimpse of what her life had been like back then. To her, recalling those festivities was a happy memory, much better than the rest of her childhood. And yet she'd been locked in her golden cage, never really living, just feeling other people's happiness from a distance.

"Make the call. We'll go," Kai stated.

And by the Goddess, Nalini would get to dance and laugh all night if she so wished. Living the festival of lights for the first time. With him.

"If we announce our intention to attend ahead of time, there's a security risk," Star pointed out, probably just so she could speak out against her brother's idea.

"It's Vratis," Evi weighed in. "Our shield there is impenetrable."

"Perhaps not for the weapon that destroyed the Nimerian base with so much ease."

He sighed, pointing to Hart. "You just told me to go." Then he indicated Star. "And you're telling me it's too bloody dangerous. Make up your damn mind, would you?"

"Giving you every aspect of an issue is kind of their job," Wench replied.

"How about crashing the party?" Nalini seemed as

surprised she'd spoken as the rest of them. "Going without announcing it ahead of time."

Evi laughed, punching her shoulder. "I knew this cabinet needed some fresh blood. Girl's smart."

"Cabinet?" she repeated.

"General of the lord's armies"—Evi pointed to herself —"and tactical advisor." Then, she waved toward the twins. "The Coats, politicians who always present different points, to make sure we see both sides of the situation. Wench is the genius, hacker, programmer, mechanic—if something needs fixing, he's on it. And Mr. Warlord. We're the brain; he's the fist. There's senators and royals who can weigh in on big questions, and local lords take care of their territories as long as they follow our laws; but the five of us basically rule this sector. As for these two," now she pointed towards Park and Ollis, who stood close to the door, "they're basically status. But they're pretty."

"She means to say," Kai corrected her, "that they're my head of security and my personal bodyguard." Then, he had to admit, "Which means they don't have much to do, yeah."

Park glared, while Ollis gave him the finger. He was lying, of course. While no one was stupid enough to actually take Kai on, the two men had plenty to do in times of war.

They piloted two light fighters always stationed at

Kai's left and right, ensuring that he was covered at all times, and blasting plenty of enemies into oblivion while they were at it.

Nalini spent a minute observing every person present with a thoughtful expression. Kai would have given a lot to know what thoughts passed behind those eyes. As usual, her shields were lowered, and she broadcasted her thoughts carelessly, but they were too jumbled up, confusing, for him to read them well.

"I probably shouldn't be lingering here then. I'm sure everything you're saying is top secret."

It was. And yet...

"I trust you, little lady," he said. "Or you wouldn't have made it on this platform."

She pouted, quite adorably, too. "I'm not ten anymore, you know. You don't have to call me *that* all the time."

Yes. That, he certainly did know.

"You're still little," he countered with a shrug, earning himself a glare.

Adorable.

Feeling the looks the members of his cabinet sent his way, he turned away. "Feel free to 'linger' if you wish. Or you could make yourself useful."

She lifted a brow, along with Evi. Wench just shook

his head, smiling knowingly. The little shit knew how long he'd looked for her, and, no doubt, could guess Kai would do just about anything to keep her next to him. Even invent a damn job for her.

"Yeah, sure." Through the reflection on the window, he saw her bite her lip. "I mean, I'm not exactly sure how I could—"

Her sentence was interrupted by visual and audible alarms flaring, alerting them of an imminent danger.

Kai returned to the control platform in the middle of the bridge. The artificial intelligence had already cleared their previous screen, displaying their attackers instead. A hologram showed a couple of hundred light fighters, white and orange—loyalists.

They were no threat to the Dominion. None of their weapons could pierce their shields. Still, Kai wasn't one to miss an opportunity, should it present itself.

"Kai?" Evi asked.

He smiled. Finally. He recognized the command ship – the largest they owned. This was their last stand.

"Crush them. Crush them all now."

His general started to give orders as he headed out of the bridge, Sky on his heels, calling the rest of his team through his comm. Before he exited the doors of the bridge, he looked back, dreading what he would see. Nalini would, no doubt, resent his bloodlust, call him out for being the barbarian he truly was at heart.

She was looking at him, all right. Walking toward him, in fact.

In her hands was the mask he'd left behind on the captain's chair. She didn't say a thing, simply handed it to him.

Kai laughed as he pulled her by the hand and bent his tall frame down to reach hers. Then he took her mouth, his lips brushing hers. Every world in the galaxy seemed to spin around their axis in that short, yet endless second. His tired, frazzled mind, body, and soul came alive, forever changed.

He managed to pull himself away, safe in the knowledge that when he returned, he'd take those lips again. And again, and again.

THIRTY

IN COMMAND

Du... uring an attack, the bridge wasn't the quiet sanctuary it had been each time she'd ventured there. It was abuzz with a purposeful energy. And she didn't belong.

Nalini was in the way of someone important wherever she stepped. Instinctively, she stuck close to Evi at first. The general was busy, so she didn't dare interrupt her.

She saw Hart and Star standing close, just as useless as she, so she tiptoed their way.

"Can I do anything?" she asked of them. Before they had a chance to answer, another question came to mind, and she added, "Is the ship safe? Kronos, the kid I came with, is down in his classroom."

Hart smiled. "We couldn't be safer. Nothing the loyalists possess can pierce our shields. The only reason we're meeting them head-on right now is to get rid of them once and for all. We came to help against the Imperials, and this is how they thank us. These people who attack us now? They'll never stop. If there's to be peace, we need to get rid of them."

Nalini would have disagreed, in general. War never created peace. Still, they were going against the loyalists.

"Oh, they need killing," she agreed.

As Krane had asked her to, Nalini had listened to their leaders' minds. She'd seen how they treated their own soldiers, she'd seen their slaves. Some of the soldiers may be innocent, but Nalini was all for obliterating their power-hungry, tyrannical filth from the galaxy. And if that made her a monster, so be it.

She was about to say just that when the floor trembled under her feet. The lights blinked on the bridge. Everyone stilled.

Fuck. This was a hit, a bad one, too. Hart had seemed so certain the shields would hold, she hadn't questioned it.

"Impossible," Wench whispered.

Evi was quicker to come to a conclusion. "Someone is messing with our shields from the inside. Dammit, Kai shouldn't have gone to help these rats."

Of course. The soldiers they'd saved, some were

completely wrapped around the loyalists' doctrines. Evi armed herself with blasters stocked inside one of the walls and threw weapons to her men.

Shit. This was her fault. She could have – should have – seen it.

Since her arrival, she'd been so preoccupied with petty little selfish concerns, she hadn't so much as opened her mind or meditated once. She hadn't tried to see anything.

Nalini had genuinely expected that Kai would demand she use her power to his advantage when she arrived. He hadn't, but still, she'd been so resolved against the very notion of being used, so determined against it, that she hadn't stopped to think whether she *should* make use of it here.

"Nalini."

Hearing her name called pulled her out of the funk. Turning to Evi, she pointed to her own chest, confused as to why anyone would think of her in this chaos.

"Kai said you piloted cargos. Are you any good at it?"

She shrugged. "I guess."

"I hope that is modesty. You're in charge. I don't have the time to comm someone else in. We need to go on manual and stay away from those fighters until I reactivate the shield."

She was about to protest, sure there could be better pilots available, but before she'd parted her lips, Evi's voice reached her mind.

«*You're a seer. We need to avoid getting hit again — two or three more blasts like that, and the ship is destroyed.*»

Fuck. No wonder she hadn't said that out loud; everyone would have panicked.

"Kass," Evi addressed another woman, "you're taking the upper deck cannons. Fire on the biggest threats, you hear me?"

But Kass wasn't hearing her at all. "We're letting *that* girl *pilot* the Dominion?"

"We don't have time for this. I need you on the cannons, Kass. You're the best and we won't survive if you can't keep their bombers at bay."

"I can't believe it. A regular we don't know at all? Over my dead body will I let a fuckdoll—"

Kass didn't finish her sentence. There wasn't so much as a shift of energy in the air warning any of the eighteen mages on the bridge that one of them was using any power, but Kass fell to her knees, choking on her words, her eyes widened, her skin ashen.

Evi could, and perhaps should, have attempted to intervene. Instead, she smiled.

Nalini stepped forward, head tilted, eyes golden. Mages' limbs often moved as a manifestation of their powers. Hers didn't anymore; not unless she truly pushed herself. But Kass' spirit was nothing to Nalini's; she broke it without any effort at all, not using much of her strength.

"Let us not pretend for another instant that you could stop me from doing anything I want to do here. Evi said I'm taking command. Deal with it and do your fucking job so we stay alive, okay?"

Nalini smirked and released the girl, who coughed deeply before staring at her in disbelief. Nalini ignored her, her attention on Evi.

"I'll keep her afloat until you get back. Whatever it takes."

The general tapped her shoulder as she passed her, running out.

Nalini sat in the captain's chair, and immediately an unfamiliar set of holographic controls appeared in front of her.

Nova in command. Approved.

Kai hadn't been kidding when he said he was clearing her for all levels. Damn, she really had control over the whole damn ship.

The neko, who hadn't shown his face since morning, entered the bridge and leaped on her lap, quite happy to show her some affection now that she was fucking busy. Typical. He started purring softly, and instead of chasing him away, Nalini surprised herself by finding some comfort in the rhythmic rumble. Alright. The beast could stay.

You can do this. You can do this, she repeated in her mind. Otherwise, Evi wouldn't have left her in charge, right? She would have asked Kass, or just about anyone else. If she'd read the general right, she was a psychic. She'd been able to tell Nalini could handle it.

Never had she piloted a ship of this size, but a large ship was just a large ship. A bigger version of the Whistle, no doubt with more power and flexibility.

You can do this...

«*Yes. You can.*»

Only when those words reverberated in her mind, said in a familiar male voice, did she truly start to believe it.

She engaged manual and opened her mind up. Truly opened it, lowering each of her shields to concentrated on *intaking* the energy around her.

She felt the direction of each hit coming at them. For all intents and purposes, she was the hits.

Nalini lifted their left wing a fraction, before nose-diving at full speed.

"Disengage stabilizers."

"What? Are you fucking insane?"

She was.

Through her comm, she gave everyone a heads-up, her voice resounding throughout the ship.

"Nalini Nova to crew. Everyone, hang on tight. We're in for a bumpy ride. Evi, engage exosuit."

She didn't say more, unwilling to warn the snake in their midst that their general was coming for him. Through her mind, she searched her surroundings until she'd found Evi's mind. Harsh exterior, heart of titanium, and, underneath it all, a warm center. She was easy to find.

«You're gonna need your propulsors.»

«Got it,» the general replied.

On that note, she started to dance through the sky. The Dominion twirled and advanced at full speed, only to stop suddenly while the fighters attempting to blow them to pieces failed, confused and frustrated.

"A ship that size shouldn't be able to move that way!" she heard their leader scream.

Nalini smiled. Any ship could; people just weren't crazy enough to pull that sort of shit.

«You okay, kid?» she asked Kronos, taking the time for

find him now that she'd adopted a rhythm.

«*No. Gonna be sick. You shouldn't be allowed to pilot. Ever.*»

He was just fine.

Finally, Nalini felt something switch on within the belly of the Dominion. Her comm came to life. "Done. Shields secured. Staying down to protect it, just in case, but you can stop the swaying."

"But it's so much fun," she protested.

"Nalini? Just no."

She pouted, but blew out a reluctant, "Fine."

She typed the command, putting the ship back on automatic; however, she did remain in the captain's chair. It was comfy.

Only now did she notice the stares from everyone on the bridge. They'd all put their safety belts on; the Coats stood together, firmly strapped against the wall. They all seemed like they were about to throw up. Instead, they started clapping. Even Kass, although the girl also glared.

"How are they doing out there?" she asked, finding the attention awkward.

"Well. We've lost seven fighters, the pilots of six of them safely ejected," one male posted behind her replied." Their exosuits were working just fine;

they're on their way back to the ship. Last one, dead. The enemy is attempting to flee. A hundred and seventy-two loyalist fighters destroyed, thirty-seven left."

«*Kai?*» she called directly to his mind, tentatively.

«*I'm here.*»

«*There's a large, well-shielded fighter; blue, with pointed engines, shooting green.*»

«*Eyes on it. It remains behind four light fighters.*»

She paused, trying to find the words. She would have liked to just say, "Blow it up," but that wouldn't have been fair or honest. So she settled on, «*It's your brother.*»

«*Half, at best.*» There was humor in his tone now. «*I'm on it.*»

His Lotus spun around at high speed, shooting relentlessly, without a second of hesitation. Less than a minute later, the ship was exploding. Then, he shot the male who ejected out of it.

Kai reached her mind this time.

«*For all the females he touched. Or made uncomfortable.*»

«*Thanks.*»

«*My pleasure.*»

KAI BURST back into the bridge and removed his mask. She felt a little awkward in his seat now, half expecting him to tell her to move.

He did no such thing.

"You crazy woman." He laughed. "I thought I was a decent pilot, you know."

Kai walked to her, stopped right in front of her, and bent down, like he had before leaving earlier. Her heart palpitated in anticipation. His lips only brushed her forehead now. A long buzz of current passed through her entire body, starting where he'd touched her down to her toes and leaving her breathless, weightless, thoughtless, just...less. And so much more, all at once.

It had taken her a long time to understand, but, finally, there was no more denying it. No more questioning what she felt. From the very start, the very first moment they'd met, she'd known Kai for what he was. She'd seen Darkness. She'd seen destruction. And yet, she'd needed him to live. Just live. Just keep on breathing, as though knowing, from the depth of her soul, that he couldn't cease to exist.

She'd loved him then, although she didn't quite know the meaning of that word yet. She did now.

"Their command ship is uncloaked," Kass said from

her station. "We have a shot at their high command now."

He didn't hesitate. "Kill them all."

She'd seen that in a vision a long time ago. Back then, she'd been horrified. And then she always saw herself, saying one simple word. She didn't even shout or scream. She didn't need to.

No.

That's just what she did now. "No."

Kai turned to her, glaring, belligerent. "They're threatening our very existence. Our peace."

"And us wiping them out is going to achieve what exactly? There are families in that command ship, just like there are here. And they'll remember what you choose to do today. You're either condemning us to a life of war, or undermining everything those loyalist pigs have fed their soldiers today. Your call."

Kai glared. Then he breathed. And finally, there was a sigh.

He started their comm, reaching out to the enemy's commander ship.

"We have you surrounded. My fighters are intact. My ship and shields are intact. We can crush you effortlessly." His thundering voice was almost bestial. "I'm very tempted to."

Kai then glanced at her. "This world is ours. Mages will live here, free and in peace, whether you like it or not. There will be no slaves. None. These are my terms. My only terms. If you don't like it, go live amongst the Imperials. But I tell you now, come back to this sector with an army, and I'll show you no mercy."

He closed the connection and reluctantly gave the order to let the loyalists go. Then, he turned to her, still grumpy, but not quite angry. "Happy?" he muttered.

Because that was all that mattered to him in the end. Her happiness.

How fucking stupid had she been? He'd cared, all along. She'd run from peace for fear of starting a thousand wars.

"Very much so."

"Good. Now, if no one objects, get this ship home. We have a party to crash."

Vratis had never been home.

But it could be.

Realizing he meant for *her* to carry on piloting the Dominion, she grinned at the unexpected present, input the coordinates and jumped to hyperspace.

Getting to Vratis from their previous location would take them only seven hours — most of the day — as there were many direct warp pathways leading right to Vratis across the sector. But taking into consideration the hour-long battle that had preceded the journey, and the fact that the cabinet had been in a meeting before that, everyone had had a very long day.

Evi was the first to go to catch some sleep, heading out as soon as they hit warp. When she came back, a couple of hours later, Hart and Ollis had gone off. They also came back quickly, and Park and Star went to sleep.

They just hovered around, pulling up maps, communicating in hushed tones through their comms, reading some reports.

"Are members of your cabinets always on call?" she mused, surprised.

Kai shook his head. "Hardly. We have a team at the ready, more than willing to take a shift on the bridge. Besides, we've entered the coordinates, and we're traveling at light speed. None of us are truly needed here right now."

Good point. She just didn't want to leave the bridge, not while Kai remained.

Besides, she definitely liked the captain's chair.

"We simply get a little controlling after an attack," he explained. "You should go get some sleep, though. You must be exhausted."

Nalini shook her head. "Not tired. Too wound up."

He smiled. "Was it your first battle?"

She bobbed her head enthusiastically.

"And we put you in charge of the whole damn crew," he tsked, shaking his head. "Oh well. I guess you didn't do too bad."

She rolled her eyes, knowing she'd killed it.

"I think this beast is cozying up to whoever is in the captain's chair," Kai said, pointing to the neko, who was still on her lap.

She snorted. "So he's not only evil, he's also cunning and power-hungry."

"And yet, for all his flaws, however much evil you see in his heart, you're very fond of him. What does it say about you, Nalini Nova?"

She hadn't expected him to be so...normal. Simple. Teasing her, with that disarming smile.

"It's not my fault. Evil and cunning males have evil and cunning ways of getting what they want."

"So, you suppose he could have charmed you. Bespelled you. Good theory."

"Not ruling it out."

"Or, perhaps there's also a dark part of you, little lady."

A blue light flashed on the command platform, demanding her attention. Regretfully, she pulled herself back to manual.

"We're close. Time to pull out of light speed."

Kai nodded, calibrating his comm, and then announcing that they were coming out of hyperspace, always a jarring feeling; preparing the crew for it made sense.

Her stomach dropped as the entire ship violently stopped. She was used to it, and they had the best stabilizers – much more efficient than those of her old Whistle, for sure – but still.

Nalini moved the Dominion towards the coordinates of Vratis.

She'd been in Vratis just over a year ago, when she'd met Krane. Entering the planet's atmosphere, Nalini didn't feel one way or another, but as they slowly approached the main city, her stomach dropped again, this time for a very different reason.

She knew that autumn sky. The farisle south of the main island. The torrent. She'd jumped out of the endless waterfall, only to be caught by one of the deadliest beasts on the entire planet. It had been a lifetime ago. Another time. A darker time.

Coming back here should have hurt more. Should have made her panic.

"Vratis Central to the Dominion," an automated voice called. "Transmit your clearance code."

"Clearance codes transmitted," she replied, after getting the ship to input their security clearance.

The translucent energy shield surrounding the city disappeared just long enough for them to pass, and reappeared right away.

"Welcome home," Kai told her.

And she breathed again.

NALINI HAD NEVER BEEN into clothes.

After the way she'd been kept bald from age three to age seventeen, she loved playing with her hair, adding strands of every color in the rainbow to it, sometimes coloring it all. She'd spent time learning complicated braids and knots. The one thing she'd never done was cut it. She'd had enough of that to last a lifetime.

In his effort to strip any individuality from her, Enlil had also ensured she was always dressed very simply, yet clothes, she never "got." She kept wearing whatever she could get her hands on for cheap, preferring to spend whatever extra cash she had on new propulsors, sensors, or on treats for Kronos.

Kai was going to change that if he kept this up. She might have rolled her eyes if a pretty dress had been waiting for her laid out on her bed, but he'd had a warrior's attire sent to her. A red chemise so soft to the touch, and various layers of silk, meant to be knotted at her waist. Working out where it was all supposed to go took some time. Her leather breeches were warm and so damn practical, she might have been spared a scar or two had she owned anything of the sort before. A leather and metal bustier was meant to go on top of all these pretty pieces of cloth, covering her heart. She smiled, seeing the tightly knit, thick, yet flowy, red cape she could hook on her left shoulder. The right one, because somehow, he'd known she would want her scar and its ornaments bared on display.

He'd actually left—or had his servants leave, more likely—a few different choices, which were all just as appealing, but her greedy hands went right to that odd ensemble. Observing herself in the mirror, she wondered if she'd ever looked quite so much like the person she was meant to be.

Nalini sat on her bathroom counter and painstakingly painted her face, applying makeup; the neko, who'd consented to keep her company for a time, leisurely played with the tap water, hissing discontentedly each time he splashed it.

"Don't make me mess this up," she told him, as though he would care to listen.

There was no doubt in Nalini's mind that the creature understood her every word; he just reveled in ignoring each and every one of them.

She carefully stepped away from the growing monster. This was a party, and, for once, she wanted to look the part. Copying the makeup she recalled from Tejen, she traced a star on her forehead and observed her handiwork. Rani would have approved.

She was just done when Kronos knocked. She

laughed, finding him with a band strapped to his head, like a warrior's.

"Looks like we had the same idea." She tilted her head. "You should go back, someday, you know. Finish your training."

The boy nodded. "I think I will. Someday."

He didn't spell it out, but she knew. He'd go when she was safe. When she had a home. When she didn't need him to anchor her.

"Soon," she added.

Kronos smiled. "Yes, soon."

THIRTY-TWO

A DANCE IN THE NIGHT

The palace had changed a lot in the last nine years. Kai had practically destroyed it and rebuilt it from scratch, with modern materials and a sleek, minimalist look. For that, she was grateful. She might have hated it if it had been the same walls within which she used to be caged.

A part of her wondered if that could be the very reason why he'd changed it. But that notion was just too self-centered by half, so she dismissed it.

The sound of drums making the floor vibrate beneath their feet, Kronos and Nalini ran downstairs, racing like children. She burst out of the palace, getting a kick out of the fact that instead of rushing to pull her back in, the enforcers just inclined their heads as she passed.

Freedom. This was what freedom tasted like. She could get used to it.

The streets were alive that night; there were stands where people offered grilled meats, refusing any payment on that one special day, which had very little to do with profit or greed. Celebrating just being alive and part of this world.

She ate everything. Kronos almost managed to keep up. There she was, going from one stand to the next, gorging herself like a pig, when he found her.

"Leave some room for the torrent delicacies down the street."

The words were whispered against her neck as he came from behind, entering her personal space like he had a right to stand there.

"There's always room for dessert," she retorted, turning to Kai.

He'd never looked more glorious. He wore nothing on top, and of that, Goddess Light knew she approved. No male should be quite so glorious. Carved in gold, sculpted like a god, each muscle powerful. Low on his waist, there were layers of dark fabric hanging, following his every movement. Strange that a male who'd never stepped foot on Tejen would be so adorned, in a manner so similar to their ceremonial dress. And yet not very strange at all.

"A skirt?" she teased him, and yet she approved.

Oh, Goddess Light, how she approved.

"One of us has to wear it, and I suspected you might prefer the trousers."

He knew her well, too well for a stranger. Reason should have reminded her they'd actually really only met a few days ago. Yet they hadn't. Not at all. She'd known him, most of what there was to know about him, from nine years of age, and he'd lived with her, within her, since. She'd just been too blind and stubborn to listen to what her heart had whispered.

Her eyes dipped low to his formal wear, and she smirked, wondering....

"Don't look at me like that right now, Nalini Nova."

"Or what?"

"Or I'll feel compelled to let you check for yourself whether I wear anything underneath."

She shook her head, wishing she could be annoyed. "It's quite unnerving how you effortlessly go through my shield." She attempted to glare, and failed. "I'm supposed to be good at this, you know."

He feigned shock. "You are?"

There was no reaction more appropriate than sticking her tongue out.

Teasing him shouldn't have felt quite like this, like playing with fire, yet it did. There was teasing and flirting, and then there was what they were doing right now. Playing, poking, and pulling at each other's ankles, all the while knowing that there was only one way this was going to end that night.

Nalini blushed and then recalled how he'd asked about a wife and children. Even thinking of it now, when he had only kissed her once, was true, pure insanity. She banished the very thought before he could catch it. Or so she hoped. His expression betrayed no sudden need to run for the hills before she could get clingy as hell, so there was hope.

"Come," he said, pulling her to him. "Dance with me."

So, they danced. All night, in any manner of ways. Slowly, unhurriedly, undulating against each other as the drums beat in sync with their hearts. His head dipped to her throat, and his lips dropped one hot kiss against it, making her gasp and then groan. Oh, how he made her feel with such simple touches. Not liking how he so completely got her under his power, she got to her tiptoes and claimed back the upper hand, as her teeth found his earlobe and nibbled at it. That would teach him.

But all it taught him was to growl, take her hips, turn her around, and press her against his cock, grinding on her, making her feel every glorious, hard inch of it through layers of fabric.

Too many layers. Too many people around them. At this point, she didn't think she would have cared, if the street hadn't been crawling with laughing children who shouldn't witness what she planned to do to this male. She almost begged him to sweep her away, take her to his room and lock her there, but Nalini Nova didn't beg, and Kai wasn't willing to stop this delicious torture quite yet. Instead of heading to the palace, or somewhere, anywhere with closed doors, he pulled them against the closest wall, ever so slightly away from the crowd. His hands dipped below the layers of soft material, one finding her naked, heavy breast, the other cupping her dripping sex. He teased her there, claiming her in public, marking her as his; her clothing remained in place, somehow making it all the more indecent.

Her mouth popped open, and she breathed hard against his chest.

"The instant I get you home," he whispered low, "I'm going to destroy every single thing that presumes to hide you from me and kneel at your feet. You're to be worshipped. You shall endure it."

"You'll do no such thing. I like these clothes." She didn't know how she could clearly enunciate anything in her current state, but somehow she managed, her voice low and seductive, the unfamiliar intonation of a temptress. "You'll kneel and wait for me to remove every single item from my body. Slowly."

As she felt her inner muscles strain, and panted against him, she plunged her hand inside his belted fabric, finding him bare. She grasped his enormous dick and moved her hand up and down, pressing her thumb hard, coaxing him.

"Oh, goddess, yes," were his last words; she then sealed his mouth with hers, muffling their panting and groaning.

He was so good with those infuriating hands, one pinching, caressing, massaging her breast, the other penetrating her wet folds, playing with her clit.

At long last, she couldn't hold it back anymore; her head fell back as she screamed in release.

He wasn't done yet, but she'd unhanded his cock. Nalini fully intended to remedy this unacceptable state of affairs, but before she could return to business, he'd lifted her off the ground and was carrying her to the palace, like she was no heavier than a feather. Damn brutish giant.

She should have blushed as she passed some faces she recognized, as this display was making their intention for the rest of the night quite clear. And yet, she couldn't find any timidity or shame.

Kai carried her to his room; she knew it was his, she'd seen it before. It hadn't changed much, although the walls did seem different, sleek and metallic, rather than the old stones she recalled. The bed was also much larger, and a good thing, too.

She wondered how many females had seen it.

Kai laughed. "None."

"Will you stay out of my head!"

"No," he refused unapologetically, gently depositing her on his soft mattress.

Then, as he'd said he would, Kai lowered his frame, dropping to one knee. She bit her lip, and licked it, too, extending her leg and caressing the side of his face with the tip of her toe. He took the foot in his hand and kissed it, making her laugh. Then, his lips wrapped around her biggest toe.

Kai moved her leg down.

"Clothes."

His word was a low, tense growl. A command that he gave all the while kneeling at her feet. And she obeyed, removing them just like she'd promised. Slowly.

First, she unhooked the cape and peeled the armor from her torso, leaving the long chemise split down her middle. Then she did away with the layers gathered around her waist before turning, giving him a view of her back as she removed the rest of the top. She hid her breast with one arm and turned her head over her shoulder to catch a glimpse of him. The effort it took to remain immobile was making him shake. She laughed and winked.

"You're going to regret this," he threatened darkly. "All of this."

It didn't take much for his temper to flare, and with each passing second, she poked the beast within.

"Am I?"

Taking a leaf from his book, as kneeling was apparently hot, she sat up on her knees, before bending forward and pushing her hips up. Only then did she start lowering her breeches, one inch at a time, making it last.

She laughed and turned back to Kai.

He was done. Completely, utterly done.

On his feet, his eyes blazing, he towered over her menacingly, glowering. She laughed as his hands pressed on her back, holding her in place. Then she was done laughing.

He brought his head to her hot, wet center, and relentlessly, punishingly, he attacked it. Sucked on her clit, too hard. Bit it. She yelped and started to pant. Needing....

She wiggled slightly. His hand pressed harder on her back, keeping her in place.

Kai coaxed with his tongue, lips, and teeth until she panted harder than she had after twelve laps around the stadium, and when she was close, so, so close, he stopped.

Then he started all over again.

"Son of a fucking shitty—"

A slap. Right on her left cheek. Then his teeth bit into her ass, hard.

"Silent," he growled.

She knew she deserved it, so she just laughed.

She took it all, until Kai's fingers parted her ass cheeks and he licked her there, shocking the hell out of her. Not an unpleasant sensation. Like, at all. Especially while he still played with her clit with one hand and fingered her with the other. Then one of his fingers entered her sensitive hole. Another one. Parting it. Expanding it.

"What are you ... Argh!" Her sentence ended in one endless scream as the pressure of a foreign object pushed against her ass, hard.

"I made this for you. Intended to give it to you someday soon. Looks like it'll be today."

She tried to turn, but she couldn't see what the ever-fucking hell he'd done to her. There was something—something that felt like a cock, but cold and metallic—inside her fucking asshole. Her *asshole*. He'd gone there. *Really*.

She started to move, but one of his hands returned to the small of her back, keeping her in place.

She turned her head as far as it could go and glared.

Kai smirked, moving the invasive object, slightly at first. Inside and out. Inside a little deeper, and out again. Faster. "How much are you enjoying yourself, little lady?"

Very, very much. And he knew it. If anything, her fucking soaked pussy was making that quite clear. No way was she actually saying it though. She stuck her tongue out again.

"What I will do to that tongue... later."

Kai never stopped fucking her ass with that thing, whatever it was, but his hot, hard member was suddenly at her entrance. She yelled as it pushed inside her, filling her so fucking much. Given its length and girth, it would have stretched her to the max by itself, but with her asshole full as well, she was close to breaking. Kai finally stopped fucking her ass, although he left his instrument inside her. He retreated his hips once, before pushing back inside, hard, fast, deep. The second time, she moved with him, meeting his thrust. Tears in her eyes, every single part of her skin tingling, she felt like she might just die if this ever stopped. She was howling, panting, crying, chanting wordless prayers, along with him.

Finally, it was just too much, she exploded in a million particles, tightening around him; groaning, he followed her into the abyss, coming and coming and coming inside her.

Kai dropped on her back, his body hot against hers, although he kept his weight off. Seconds, hours, years might have passed. Then, he removed the object from inside her ass. She muttered something that may very well have been a protest, and he laughed. He dropped to his side, taking her with him, then flipped her over to have her straddling him. His hips moved upward, as he hardened inside her.

"Again, now? After that?"

She could have used another minute.

Kai sat up and wrapped his lips around her left nipple as he cupped the other one, playing with it, and she realized she didn't need a minute at all.

THIRTY-THREE

THE END OF THE DREAM

"No."

"But I made it for you. It's the best fucking whip in the galaxy."

"Keep it if you like it so much."

That thing had been lodged in her fucking ass. Whatever he said about cleaning it, she wasn't going to use it.

"I'll take those instead."

Kai groaned, grumbled, and even pouted, but, in the end, he gave her his deer horned knives and kept the whip.

She soon realized relinquishing the weapon to his custody had been a mistake, as he enjoyed using its hilt on her at the first opportunity.

Other than the disagreement over the whip-slash-dildo, fitting into Kai's life was seamless, so natural she even questioned why she believed she might not have belonged there.

There was always work to be done amongst the cabinet. Questions that needed to be weighed and assessed; her opinion was paramount to any decision Kai made. They didn't always agree. In fact, most of the time, they butted heads. But truth was, no one else could challenge his ideas and decisions as she did. He listened to her. And he compromised.

The sex was all so deliciously filthy after an argument in command. And in the mornings. In the evenings, too.

There weren't many occasions that didn't demand filthy sex, she soon learned.

Kai enjoyed controlling, dominating her, as much as he enjoyed having her tell him what to do. Remaining still and taking whatever she wanted to give. Letting her suck him without being allowed to touch her.

She always paid for such torture, but it was worth it.

Her third month in Vratis, he shocked the bejesus out of her one day. For the first time since her arrival, the Council of Ratna was gathering. Not just his cabinet, but every noble and senator would be there to discuss matters. She left their bathroom to find a white and gold robe in her size left on their bed.

"You mean to have me attend? Wearing this?"

Her astonishment amused him, but she saw nothing funny.

"Evi isn't attending. Park isn't attending. Wench isn't attending. Ollie isn't attending. Only the Coats, because they're *senators*. I can't just barge in there and...."

He was leaning against the wall, smiling in an infuriatingly gorgeous and sexy way, trying, and almost managing, to make her forget why she was so mad.

"You know when I asked you if you'd seen my wife a while back?"

She froze.

"That was because I saw her. Back the very first time we met. I mean, to be fair, there were fuckloads of visions running through those beautiful eyes of yours. But I caught sight of her, and everything else faded."

Nalini frowned and, without meaning to, took a step back as she attempted to decrypt his words. When she failed to, she did what he did to her every day, shamelessly. She brushed against his mind, finding it completely open. Bared to her.

And she saw it, that vision he talked of. Her. In his arms. Smiling and pregnant and so fucking happy she cried, at a loss for words.

Feeling like someone had just punched her in the stomach, then pulled her up, given her a hug, chucked her at a wall, and started to sing her name, she sat, dizzy, disoriented, knocked off course.

"Obviously, I didn't actually realize the cute little girl in front of me would grow into you. Would have made things easier. *And* it also took me a while to gather that *you* hadn't seen that. Too busy paying attention to war, destruction, and all those pesky little details, I guess." He tsked, biting back a smile.

"Get changed, Nalini. We haven't exchanged vows. I haven't even worked out how I am to ask you to spend the rest of your life bound to me. But there is an official gathering today, and I *will* have you by my side."

He came to her, kneeling as he often did, and putting his head against her chest. Then he got up and went to the bathroom.

It was as well that he had felt that she was needed in council. If he hadn't, she wouldn't have been there when it all fell apart.

THE COUNCIL WAS HELD in a floating building, high over the city. Inside, it was circular, with rows upon rows of grandstands, so that every Coat could sit comfortably. Nalini noticed her parents, who gasped when they saw her. She kept her eyes forward, purposefully avoiding theirs. Not now.

Council, it turned out, was boring. No doubt, Kai had asked her to come so he could play footsie while they discussed taxes and trade routes. Long hours passed, and preventing herself from yawning was a hell of a challenge.

Then, all of a sudden, it started. An explosion, taking out rows of politicians, who screamed as they burned and fell into the skies of Vratis.

Kai and Nalini got to their feet, hands hooked.

It didn't help. The next blast had them both unbalanced, falling away from each other.

It had been a precise, fast, practically suicidal attack.

First, came the bombs, sounding far too close for comfort; whatever technology had been used, it had hit their shield, she could tell.

Nalini froze, completely shocked; she hadn't seen this. This time, she'd been looking. Every day, she took the time to meditate and yet this attack took her completely by surprise.

Nalini didn't have the time to wallow in disappointment and guilt, however. Now it had all started, she could help.

She leapt to her feet. Kai was giving evacuation

orders to his troops; rather than trying to explain herself, she just stood towards the left side of the chamber, and yelled, "All of you, get down on the ground immediately, arms covering your head."

She was relieved to see that over half of the Coats obeyed. Seconds later, a bomb hit.

Most of those who had listened to her lived. Practically all of those who'd ignored her, however, were killed either by the blast or the fall of large pieces of ceiling and walls flying around.

Soldiers wearing black and purple exosuits, imperial colors, were flying down from the hole in their shield at high speed. Still in the sky, but close enough for her to read their minds.

These were their enemy's best fighters, and they'd been sent with one goal, one single focus in mind.

She saw more.

No fucking wonder she hadn't seen this coming.

She turned to Kai.

"Listen to me. You're going to hate this, but you have to go now. I have to be alone. They'll take me, and go. That's their one mission."

Nalini saw it in their minds. Knowing that they had orders to do whatever it took to bring her, *her,* alive, she did what she had to.

"No way," Kai replied, shaking his head to emphasize his refusal.

"Yes, way," she protested. *"Trust me."*

He glared at her for a long time, before dropping his forehead on hers, and holding it there.

Then, he was gone.

The enemy soldiers were down in no time. Nalini held her hands up, in show of surrender, and let them take her.

Kai could have stopped it at any point. He was close, so close, watching them from the shadows. He could have destroyed them all. He wanted to

«*You better be fucking right about this.*»

She was.

WHILE SHE WAS TAKEN in a transport heading up to the imperial command ship, Nalini scanned every soldier within range. They really ought to train them to keep their thoughts to themselves, if they were supposed to fight against mages. She had no problem identifying the perpetrators of this attack; the soldiers thought of them constantly, wondered if they'd be rewarded for a job well done.

There were seven minds behind this. Six strangers

and one person she knew. One person she and Kai both knew.

Ian Krane.

Everything Krane said or did was purposeful, she knew that now. He'd befriended Kai at the first opportunity, only to leave him and seek her out. Then, when he'd found her, he'd convinced her to follow him the only way she would have accepted. Then, he'd been wise enough to send her to Nimeria, first, rather than launching her into Kai's arms. He was always one step ahead.

One thing didn't make any fucking sense, however. He'd spent a thousand years away from the Wise; he'd said so himself. And suddenly, he was joining them?

Somehow, he all made sense.

What had he said again, when they'd parted ways? *I'm going to be right in a viper's nest, and I could use an ally.*

The old male was moving pieces in a game, and only he knew the rules. The one question was, whose side was he on? Hers and the rest of their kingdom, or the Imperials'?

There was no indubitable fact that could have irrefutably proven his loyalty. And yet...

He was on their side. He cared about her, and about

Kai. About them all. This was the one truth she knew about Ian Krane.

Now, it was just a matter of figuring out what role she was supposed to play in his deadly games.

SHE'D SPENT a year with him in Tejen, where there was so much for a mage to learn, so many different facets to explore. And yet, Krane had only been interested in two things: strengthening her shields and make her understand bonds.

Shields and bonds...

It all meant something. She strained against fear, disentangling the maze of her mind.

Shields and bonds....

And, quite suddenly, she knew.

Her shields would allow her to navigate amongst vipers. They'd never know her inner thoughts, her true loyalty. She could show them what they wanted to see and hide the rest. She could lie. She was strong enough to.

As for the bond...

Nalini had often had her shields in place, and yet, she'd somehow been able to communicate with Kai by sharing thoughts directly through to his mind, as clearly as if she'd spoken them out loud, yet only heard by him. Thoughts Evi and other psychics couldn't get access to.

There was a strange bond linking them, connecting their minds, and it was impenetrable and inaccessible to anyone else.

The moment these two facts clicked, she knew what matter of pawn she was meant to be.

ONCE THEY REACHED the Imperial command ship, she was taken to a tall, beautiful, green-haired Wise, a member of the Council. Perhaps the most cunning amongst them.

"Nalini Nova. We meet at last."

Nalini tested her theory out.

"Thanks for getting me out. I didn't think I'd ever be free of these monsters."

Her shields firmly in place, she thought of all the ways she'd dismember the smiling female in front of her. Kovak's mind was scanning hers, they both knew it. Yet her smile never faltered.

"Oh, poor girl. Come, come. Tell me what happened to you."

It had worked. Easily. She smiled, conveying her gratefulness, and followed the snake into the belly of her ship.

Telling her story took some time. Then she had to answer the questions.

"Yes, Master Krane recommended I seek the loyalists after Tejen," she informed them. "He thought I'd be safe from *them* there."

Kovak probed around her shields again. Nalini let her old memories pass through. Her fear of Kai, of being hunted and locked away.

The Wise smiled.

"But you weren't. Kai Lor attacked the base."

No, the Imperials had attacked the base, probably on Kovak's order, she now realized. Killing hundreds, if not thousands, of innocents to lure Kai's armies out. The Imperials had been behind the loyalists' attack on the Dominion right after they'd come to help the survivors of Nimeria. They'd attempted to hide in the shadows while the Ratnarians took each other out, rather than officially getting involved. Pure hatred in her heart, Nalini nodded and managed to fake a sniffle.

And unbelievably, the ageless, all-powerful creature before her fell for it. For her lie.

«*Kai.*»

This was the ultimate test. Could she really speak to him from so far away, and without anyone else detecting it?

Immediately, she felt his presence. Concealing her relief and happiness took some effort.

«You're alive.»

She didn't simply hear his words; she could also feel his emotions, his fear and apprehension, his relentlessness. He hadn't really doubted it. If she'd died, he would have felt it, known it to his core. Still, hearing her voice was a relief he desperately needed. She wished she could tell him she was coming back right away.

«I am.»

He'd just trust her because she'd asked, but she knew he was desperate for an explanation. She didn't have much time, but she tried to clarify the situation.

«They wanted me, and they had that weapon they used on Nimeria at the ready. They would have used it on every single defenseless surrounding system while we hid behind our shield. This was the only way. They would have taken me, and used me as they saw fit. Now, it looks like I came voluntarily. That changes things.»

«How? What do they want from you?»

«I don't know how yet, but I feel their intention. They mean to use me as a weapon. Against you.»

«How's that working out for them?»

She hid a smile and kept on telling Kovak all she wanted to hear.

She couldn't afford to start an onslaught on the elder's mind, but she still brushed against it, ever so softly, almost teasing it, trying it for a taste.

Kovak felt victorious. She truly believed she'd won.

«*Oh, it's working pretty well, in their minds, at least. I'm serving shit and my minder is eating it up.*»

«*That's my girl.*»

Yes, she was.

«*Nalini, where are you? I'll come get you. We can take out their weapon.*»

He wasn't going to like her plan. Not at all.

«*On their ship. They're taking me to Magneo. And you can't stop it.*»

There was a short silence followed by a trail of curses that made her smile. Kovak smiled back, believing it was meant for her, an expression of gratitude after she'd saved Nalini from the big, bad Kai.

«*Listen to me. I can talk to you. From the other end of the galaxy, I can talk to you. And no one realizes it.*»

«*So?*»

«*So, this is what we need, Kai. You could come save me, blow that bitch out of the sky, and then what? The*

Council will just send another crazy on our ass, and another one after that. Blood and fire, now until the end of time.»

«So be it.»

«Stop being such a guy! Kai, they trust me. For some crazy reason, they think I'm their key. I can get there and unravel them from the inside. Send you everything I know. The location of their weapons, their bases, their numbers. Everything we need.»

«You mean to be a spy.»

«I mean to be a weapon. This ends now, Kai.»

He knew she was right, and it was killing him to admit it.

His terms were simple.

«Check in when you can. If it's risky, don't. Don't take unnecessary risks. You find yourself in danger, you get out and call for help.»

«Obviously.»

The tall, green-haired Wise was telling her about Magneo, the emperor, and a bunch of other shit Nalini didn't give any crap about. But she let a memory of happiness and safety pass through her shield, and Kovak kept going, believing every single lie she'd woven.

"Everyone will be so delighted to have you with us,

Nalini. With you, we have a chance to finally end this, once and for all."

"Yes. Finally."

This time, she wasn't lying at all. She fully intended to end this war.

"What do you mean she's infiltrated the enemy?" There was a dark edge to Evi's words. "She's no soldier. No enforcer. No nothing."

Kai's glare cut through to his general, but what he saw stayed his hand. Worry. Evi wasn't undermining Nalini's aptitudes, as much as worrying on her behalf.

"She can handle this. Trust me."

That was the one reason why, against his every instinct, he'd let her do what she'd proposed to do. She could handle this.

"What the hell? They could kill her there, or worse."

Kai turned his back on his general, returning to his

window. Watching the infinity of space always calmed him. Today, it didn't work.

"We should go get her out of there before it's too late—"

"Evi," Hart interrupted. "Have you ever seen Nalini afraid?"

The general paused.

Park nodded, agreeing with the Coat, and adding, "I practically pissed myself on my first raid. She was in the bridge, taking over command when you and Kai were busy elsewhere, and damn, the way she flew this ship? Never seen anything like that, before or since."

Kai smiled. It had been some damn fine flying, that was for sure.

"And let's not forget how she, a tiny little waif, almost won against Kai in a fucking fist fight."

"Yeah, he actually had to break his own damn arm to take the upper hand," Ollis reminded them, shaking his head as if he still couldn't believe it.

A smile flashed at the recollection. Kai was pretty certain the only reason he'd won was because his move had shocked the heck out of her.

"She can handle this. And if she couldn't, Kai would be on his way to get her back already."

He was tempted to go regardless; although she'd kick his ass for ruining her crazy-ass plan.

Finally finding his words, he returned to the command console, purposefully staring down Evi before turning to the rest of the cabinet.

"Every day, I fight for this kingdom of ours and no one blinks. Let your queen fight for what's hers."

A long silence followed this. Queen, he'd said. Not consort or wife—because she was neither. She'd proved as much today.

SEVEN MINDS, all strong, all pushing hers, willing it to fall.

Well, six of them were pushing. Ian Krane, seated at the very center of the half-circular table, the place of honor, wasn't attempting to invade her mind. Instead, he sent her a knowing smile and a wink. He wasn't even hiding it. The others saw it and assumed he was congratulating her for making the right choice, returning to their side.

Nalini knew better.

She recapped her life, purposefully letting them see glimpses that gave truth to her lies. Kronos in her arms, her cursing Kai, telling him it was all his fault.

She always wanted to flinch when she recalled doing that, but she sold it well.

The lies truly started when she'd come aboard the Dominion, but by that point, they had enough proof. No reason to doubt her.

"When Kovak's men came, I saw in their minds that they meant to offer me asylum, and I leaped at the chance."

She'd leaped, all right.

The Wise Council exchanged glances and finally nodded. "You did well, Kovak. And, Nalini, you'll be very safe here, from now on."

Rator Main, the dark-blue-skinned Evris who spoke, meant every word, but she couldn't quite see what purpose they had for her yet. She knew it concerned Kai, that she was the piece they needed to destroy him, but how remained to be seen. No matter. She could wait. She hadn't expected all the answers in her first hour here.

"We shall discuss a course of action amongst ourselves, child," said Rator. "Go anywhere you please in this complex. You're safe."

That word again. They truly were trying to drill that notion into her for some reason.

Nalini wasn't surprised that they'd given her freedom. How could anyone truly test her intention without observing her doing as she pleased?

She didn't lift her head to see the cameras on every ceiling, and the drones flying by if she ever stepped too far from their range. She knew they were there, recording her every move, but blatantly looking at them would have seemed conspicuous. Nalini made her way through the building until she'd found a balcony giving her a view of Magneo.

It truly was an enchanting place, even to one who'd seen Tejen; but where everything had seemed natural and in balance back there, Magneo was a pretty, handcrafted picture. Bright, overly vibrant, with pink bushes and fluorescent fountains.

She leaned forward, pretending to bask in its beauty, and made the connection.

«*I'm there. It's pretty.*»

She shared a flash of the landscape before her eyes.

«*Looks like a unicorn puked all over it.*»

She tried not to snort.

«*We arrived in the main hangar. There's a hundred landing platforms, all guarded by two squadrons. Our ship was small and low risk, yet we were followed by a dozen fighters. They take their security fucking seriously.*»

«*So they should.*»

«*The Imperial palace is linked to the main hangar; there's a tunnel leading there. The Wise live in a separate building. That's where I am now. There's only a few guards, and the seven members of the council in this building. Our old friend is among them.*»

Kai paused.

«*You're surrounded and guarded.*»

He didn't like it. Nor did she.

«*For now.*»

«*For now,*» he agreed.

She let the link go, feeling the approaching Evris, the one who'd introduced herself as Flara Duchey.

"Magnificent, is it not?"

"Truly."

If one favored unicorn puke.

"It's dangerous out there when the sun goes down. There's many wild creatures in these woods."

She wondered if they, too, had been painted pink.

"Let me show you to your quarters, child."

She hadn't failed to note how fucking condescending they always were with her, calling her a child and patting her hand like Flara did just then.

She would have loved to see their faces when they realized the child had destroyed everything they held dear, but she planned to be fucking far away from them by the time they understood she'd played them.

NALINI WOKE up to a copper android informing her in its robotic voice that breakfast was ready. She stretched before getting out of bed and popping into her advanced, sleek bathroom.

Coming back, she found the machine standing at the exact same spot where she'd left it.

"Well, lead the way."

The android took her to an elegant dining room decorated in white and blood blue; all the Wise council members were seated around the table.

"Ah. Come, come. Take a seat."

She obediently went to occupy the place Kovak was patting, next to her.

"I trust you slept well."

She had. She'd slept feeling Kai next to her all night long. He'd been so bold as to tease her nipples, taking them in his mouth, from half a galaxy away. A smile on her face, she nodded. "Never better. I'm truly glad to be here. I hope I'll be able to help."

Translation: tell me how you mean to use me.

The Wise exchanged that look again. She itched to try to breach their filthy minds and see what they meant by it, but it just wouldn't work with the naive and slightly dumb role she was playing.

"And you will," Krane said, his blue eyes boring into hers. "Soon."

She got the message loud and clear. *Patience, little lady.* Too bad that had never been her forte. She had to push it.

"Great. I was pretty much kept in one room the whole time, but I'm sure I have intel to share. About the Dominion, Vratis, and all."

She'd lie through her teeth, sprinkling it all with a bit of truth; then she'd rush to tell Kai exactly what she'd revealed, so he could make sure to be ready to act consequently.

But the Wise spared her the bother. They were laughing.

"We're not concerned about that ship or that little planet, girl," said Rator. "Our StarX can destroy an entire fleet of Dominions in minutes. Or destroy an entire city. The problem isn't killing Kai Lor. He's nothing but the one shell a true blight has used this time around. What our order needs to do is put an end to that blight."

Food tasted like ash in her mouth. She had a hard time swallowing it.

"What do you mean?"

"You know of Darkness. A long time ago, using the dark, terrible magic it wields, it ensured its ability to return to our world, even after death."

She nodded. She knew as much; that explained Kai. The prophecy said Darkness would return.

"So, if we kill Kai, after his death, Darkness will form again, and again, and again. This circle of death will never end."

She nodded, wanting more. Needing more.

"Right. How do you stop it?"

"We couldn't," Krane replied, putting his fork down. "Not without you. I don't suppose you understand; you never were very good at detangling all these visions."

She sent him a pointed glare, as he winked and removed his glove, leaving it next to his cutlery. Nalini frowned as she tried to recall seeing him without gloves, and came up blank. Slowly and carefully, she moved her hand across the table and wrapped it around his.

Ian Krane opened his tightly bound, closed mind to her for the fraction of a fleeting instant.

And then, she saw *everything*.

Not simply visions. Memories, clear ones. She saw the face of a girl who bore an expression so dark and fierce.

"Kai, as female," she said, unsurprised. She'd seen as much in her vision, a long time ago.

"Yes, he was, in that first life. And since, he's been reborn many times, in the shape of a male and a female. Male, more often than not, of course."

Of course, because for every two Evris males, only one female was born. Over sixty percent of their population was male. She hadn't seen any stats on this, but it seemed to her that females were even rarer amongst mages. She'd seen perhaps five males for every female, in Kai's rank, and back on Tejen.

Male or female, he was recognizable. The same eyes. The same focus and determination.

It didn't end just there though. That female who so many called Darkness smiled sometimes. Softly, sadly, fleetingly, but she smiled still. Always at the same person. A male with eyes Nalini knew. She'd seen them in the mirror often enough.

"Okay, *I'm* a guy. That's weird."

She grimaced, feeling a little queasy.

"What happened?" she asked Ian, as he removed his hand before she could see it.

"Darkness was about to do something that would have killed a hell of a lot of people. So, you killed her."

Time seemed to stop the moment he said it. Nalini shook her head and opened her mouth to deny it. She would have loved to, but she couldn't.

Of course she had. Everything made sense to her now. Her fear at the start. She wasn't one to run from danger, not really.

Running away from the responsibility of killing him, though? Hell yes. Hiding at the end of the universe to not have to ever do that sounded like a good plan to her.

"And then?"

"And then, you died. I was there back then. The moment you passed, I had that vision. Quite clear. Very, very much a prophecy. So, I wrote it down."

And the rest of the Wise decreed that no mage should ever be born, to avoid fulfilling it. It worked for a thousand years or so, until now. Until Kai.

"I don't really understand what it all has to do with killing Darkness for good."

"Darkness," said Rator, "isn't the only thing coming back through time."

Oh.

Her. She stiffened.

"So, you want to kill me, too."

More condescending laughter.

"That would be quite counterproductive, child. When Darkness died, each time through the ages, you've perished along with it. And when it is reborn, shortly after, you're also brought back to life. Darkness has created a circle where she and her Light could meet again. There's one easy way to break that circle for good. Ensure that when Darkness perishes, this time, you, his Light, stay alive. If you're not reunited beyond death, we have every reason to believe that Darkness won't be able to come back."

She was getting a headache, attempting to understand it all.

Ian translated that statement. "We're gonna make you immortal, kid."

And then, they'd send their machine and destroy Kai.

A good plan. A great plan, in fact.

And it might have worked if they hadn't shared it with her.

They'd planned her operation that very day, and there was no way to stop it without blowing her cover. Nalini was accompanied by one of the sniveling elders everywhere for hours, making her want to scream. She needed time alone, to explain everything to Kai as best she could.

He could feel her distress through the bond.

«*What's wrong?*»

«*I'm fine.*»

A lie, and he could tell.

«*Nalini...*»

«*I'm safe.*»

Truth this time. She was about to get so fucking safe.

Immortal. Practically impossible to destroy. They'd

explained it to her. If she cut herself, the wound would heal in seconds. She cut off her foot, it would regrow as long as she didn't bleed out. The only way to kill her would be to make sure that her body was completely destroyed in one blow, too quickly for the microscopic nanocytes inside her to reform her organs. Decapitation. *Maybe* a well-placed blow to the heart, they weren't sure. No immortal had ever died of one. Burning them to a crisp could work, if it was fast enough.

«*They're shooting you with nanocytes.*» He'd discerned that through her jumbled thoughts. «*Is it the immortality serum?*»

«*Yes.*»

«*Good.*»

Of course, he liked the idea of her being that durable.

Smiling so hard her face could split in two, as she talked with Kovak about the challenge of keeping their hair colored for more than a few weeks, she tried to explain.

«*Not good. Once it's done, they'll kill you. With their damn weapon. It's called StarX – look up what you can about it. A cold fusion reactor they've tested against a dying star, Kai. It can blast through any shield.*»

«*When?*»

«*I don't know. Today, maybe. I won't let them do this.
I'll kill them all.*»

«*You will* not *put yourself in harm's way. We had a
deal, remember? Stay safe.*»

«*I can't.*»

She couldn't watch him die, even if he could come
back. And there was a real chance he wouldn't.

«*You and I, we come back to life together. Always.
And making me immortal is a way to ensure you stay
trapped in whatever world lies after this. After life.*»

Seconds passed without a word.

«*Yes. I see that now. You and I. I'd brave death to
return to you.*»

He had, again and again.

Now was probably not the time to tell him he'd been
a girl though.

«*Listen to me, Nalini. Whatever they do, they won't
win. They won't stop me from coming back. If there's
consciousness after life, I'll find a way.*»

But she didn't want to lose him... and there was more.

«*Wench. Evi. Park. Ollis. Hart. Star. Kronos. Sky.*»

She just kept on giving him the names of everyone he
loved, hurting him, but making him see reason
—she hoped.

«You forget. I am Darkness.»

He said nothing else, but what he meant was clear.

Let them all burn, if we must. This was who he was at heart. Who he'd always be. And she loved him nonetheless. So much.

Loving him enough to come back to life for him hadn't stopped her from killing him the first time around. Just as Darkness would remain Darkness, she'd always be Light. Always remain on the side of life and peace.

No wonder the council believed her crap. She'd given them every reason to trust that she'd do what was needed of her to keep the peace.

But they'd failed in their machinations this time. Failed to manipulate *her* as they saw fit.

A year ago, they might have won. If they'd taken her while fear and prejudice had dwelled in her heart, they could have made her theirs again.

Instead, Ian Krane had dropped her right in the middle of it, where she could take a long, hard look at the world and see the truth.

Darkness was cold, sometimes even cruel. There were so many words one might use to describe him. If she had to settle on one, however, she would have said that Darkness was *good*.

Slavery, to which the Imperials and Council turned a blind eye, was gone in their sector. Children weren't killed for the simple sin of possessing power.

But he'd just admitted to a terrible truth: his willingness to forsake everyone else.

If he had to choose between her and the galaxy, Kai would choose her. This was his one sin. And a sin he wouldn't need to commit, if she was by his side. Safe.

The Council, however, never was true, not even to themselves.

They'd lost their way a long time ago, when they'd condemned that poor innocent woman and forged her into Darkness. They'd been moved by fear. Fear of power. For what proof did they have that she would indeed bring any form of destruction? At that point, she'd only made use of her power to save her people.

No, they'd seen her power and realized that it surpassed theirs, a thousand times. A trillion times. That she could seize power and take it for herself.

Their sin was a lust for power. Kai's sin was love.

The Council of Wise were the true enemy. They always had been.

Nalini closed her eyes and saw that vision that had haunted her since she was ten years of age. Kai, hand outstretched, destroying a star. Her, by his side, holding his hand.

«*I know how this ends,*» she informed him.

«*Not with your death.*» That was no question, but a promise.

«*Nor yours. It ends with theirs. It ends with us destroying their world. It ends in strands of Starfire.*»

«*I like the sound of that. What are we doing?*»

So, she told him, as she was taken down to the labs and made into an immortal.

Ian Krane hovered over her, watching her on the operating table. He took her hand.

"Not gonna lie. It's going to hurt for a bit. You'll sleep through it."

She nodded. "Don't let them start without me. I want to be there. When they go to destroy Darkness, I want to help if I can. And I want to see my enemies burn."

He smiled at her.

"Proud of you, kid. More than you know."

He squeezed her hand as the other members of the council circled around their weapon like vultures.

"Thank you," she said, as the doctor inserted a needle at the back of her neck.

Her veins were fire and ice. She screamed until they finally forced her to sleep.

———

THE DREAM WAS PEACEFUL. It shouldn't have been. She dreamed of fire and death.

THE VERY GROUND was falling beneath their feet. The planet had minutes, at most. She needed to get off there. Now. Instead, she ran. To a woman.

And Nalini knew she was a male in this life. A male called... Elnur.

It mattered not. Flesh and blood were nothing. The only thing she knew was love.

He ran to Phne, the female he lived and breathed for, and when her eyes saw him, she gasped in terror. She looked past him and saw a speeder. Exhaling in relief, Phne pointed to it. "Please go. Leave now. This is my doing. My nightmare."

Her path had led her here, to his burning world; Elnur's choices were the opposite. He'd earned peace. He'd earned the right to live, dammit.

"Come with me," Elnur countered.

She shook her head.

"I need to stay here and keep this furnace from exploding until everyone is evacuated." Phne strained to speak, desperate to make him understand.

Elnur knelt next to Phne and took her hand.

"You need to leave."

"I literally can't without you. I got it all wrong, Phne. From the start. The Council has tricked me and lied. You aren't going to destroy worlds. You aren't going to kill gods." He rolled his eyes, half laughing, half crying. "All along, that was all about us. We're the Goddess Light. The Goddess of Darkness and her Light. This damn prophecy they used to condemn you was never about war and destruction. It was about us coming together and ruling this world. It was about our race not needing the Council's bullshit anymore."

Phne stared into his eyes, not understanding a word; because if she did understand, it would make everything so much worse.

She'd believed those words. She'd believed she was Darkness and nothing else. Destruction. And she'd acted accordingly.

Yet what should have been insane sentiments was resonating in her, somewhere deep down.

"It's too late," she cried. "This planet is going to explode. It's too close to the star. The entire system is doomed. And every transport leaving right now will blow. I need to save them. And you need to go, El."

"Never."

Phne started to cry as he took her hand.

"I'll come back. We both will. Someday, we'll meet again. And I'll save you this time. I should have been there, standing right next to you, against them. Let the universe burn in Starfire if I had to. You saved my life, Phne. And since that day, a part of me has belonged to you. It always will."

Elnur's comm device, still working, came to life and a voice confirmed the evacuation was complete.

Phne heard it. She smiled.

The planet was unstable as ever; neither of them could stop the inevitable for much longer. El's speeder had been destroyed long ago; they hadn't even looked at it.

It didn't matter now, in the end. Nothing mattered anymore. They were together.

Phne let go of her hold on the planet core as her lips descended on Elnur's, taking them in one last, desperate, white-hot kiss.

They'd meet again. And again and again, until the end of time. They were true mates, their souls bound to each other.

That was his last thought as he prepared himself for death.

NALINI WOKE WITH A START. Her body was disgustingly wet with sweat, her heart beating hard, and her face salted with dry tears.

«*Kai...*»

He needn't say a word: she felt it. Her dream, he'd seen it all.

«*Mate,*» was his one-word confirmation.

They'd waited.

She sighed in relief, knowing it was no doubt Ian Krane's doing. The humongous, spherical starship they meant to use as a weapon just so happened to be ready right when she awoke. Having another seer in her corner rocked.

The Wise all went on board, unwilling to miss their moment of triumph.

"Nalini, dear, you're certain you're well enough?" Kovak asked sweetly.

She smiled and nodded. "I want to see it. I was kidnapped. I want to see it burn."

Lie and truth, all wrapped in one, presented with a pretty bow.

"Very well." Kovak patted her hand.

She wasn't allowed on the deck here. These people meant to coddle her and treat her like a small, breakable object, even after making her indestructible. She had a hard time not rolling her eyes, although being away from them, and mostly left alone with just two guards, certainly served her purpose.

Feeling that the ship had exited light speed, she moved, quiet, efficient, lethal. Two flips of her wrists, and the guards fell, necks snapped. She moved the bodies into her room, and was on her way.

Nalini had two missions. One of them she took from their book.

It was handy to have a traitor aboard, when one wanted to mess with your shields.

«We've arrived in the sector. I don't have the coordinates yet, bear with me,» she informed Kai.

She encountered a few enforcers, none of which paid her any mind. Being underestimated at every turn did, in fact, help.

She got to a computer and pulled up the information she needed, sending it to Kai.

«Got it. Just find a transport and get out of there. Come to me,» he commanded.

«Not yet. We don't know how strong their shield is, but I'd put my money on very. Let me mess with it.»

«*Nalini...*»

«*And I need to find Krane. I'm not sure he knows we mean to blow this joint.*»

Kai swore. Then he was resigned, knowing arguing would have been pointless. «*Alright. Hurry, and confirm when you're out of there. We're coming.*»

She knew the moment they'd jumped to their location; it helped her locate the source of the weapon's shield, as the Wise engaged them as soon as the Dominion appeared on their radar.

Following the source of the energy, she ran. It might have been the Imperial uniform she wore, or the Wise orders, but no one stopped her. Finally, she opened a door, and...

The shot should have killed her. Would have the day before. It was precise. Went right through her heart.

«*Nalini.*» Kai's tone was urgent.

Kovak laughed. "You're good, sweetheart. I'll give you that."

Nalini coughed her guts up, struggling to breathe, to stay awake. Tears streamed down her face.

"Just not good enough."

The kicks started, hard, on her flank.

"Did you really think you could fool me? I'm a thousand, three hundred years old. I was there when you and that filthy shit tried to seize the power the first time. I saw your eyes then. I see them now."

Another kick, this time breaking her nose.

«*Nalini!*» Kai screamed helplessly through their bond.

She wanted to tell him she was there still. Holding on. Alive, for now. But any communication now might make things worse. He'd remember her words. Her last words.

Kovak lifted her blaster again and took aim.

A blast fired. Nalini looked death in the eyes.

Kovak fell back, shocked, one word on her lips. "You..."

Following the direction where the Wise stared, Nalini turned her head and saw a tall figure. A wolf. Salt and pepper hair.

"Me, you piece of shit. Guess you should have looked at my eyes."

Kovak wasn't dead; the nanocytes inside her body had started to heal her, just like they healed Nalini, so she'd expected Ian to shoot her again. Wanted him to.

He did no such thing. No, Ian was too much of a sadistic motherfucker for that.

"Nox. Take care of her, will you?"

Nox was no dog, he didn't take orders, unless he felt like it. Right now, he did.

The wolf pounced on the woman's head and ripped out her throat.

Okay. She'd needed killing, badly, but Nalini was going to throw up nonetheless.

She needed to do one thing. Immediately. Focusing took some effort, but she managed. «*I'm alive. Krane. Krane came through.*»

«*Fuck. Don't you ever do that again.*»

«*Don't plan to.*»

"Trust me when I say she deserved worse, kiddo," Ian said, moving to the control platform at the middle of the room, disabling the shield. "Come on. Let's get out of here. I need you to stay with me, long enough to tell your mate you're out of here in a few, okay? Then you can pass out."

The old male picked her up, throwing her over his shoulder.

"Okay? Stay awake, stay awake, stay awake," he chanted. "Want me to sing? My singing is terrible. Should keep you conscious. Don't answer that. Talking would hurt like hell right now."

He spoke to her all the way to the escape pod, making her wish laughing wasn't so damn painful.

"We're out."

She repeated the information to Kai, and immediately he deployed his fighters. She saw it through the small window.

It wouldn't be enough against this machine. She knew just what it needed. *«Where are you?»*

He answered immediately. *«The bridge. I'm not fighting. I need to see you.»*

Krane directed the escape pod inside the Dominion and held her up, half carrying her.

"The bridge. I need—"

"Sleep. You need to sleep it off. Trust me on this."

"Kai. I need..."

Fast steps approached, and there he was, right in front of her, holding her in his arms; although it hurt, she pulled him tight, crying against his chest. She'd almost died. She'd almost lost him.

"Never. You'll never lose me. I thought you'd get that by now. I'd die along with you, and we'd meet again."

"Let's just not do that, though," she begged through her tears.

"Seconding that request," Krane supplied.

Both she and Kai turned to him. Kai put one hand on his shoulder, and Nalini took his arm.

"Dude, tell me we're not doing hugs," Krane sighed. "I can't deal with it. Don't even have tissues."

He wasn't one to show affection. Feeling it, however....

All of a sudden, the veil was lifted, revealing what he'd hidden behind his wall.

"You were my father," she said.

Or he had been, at the very beginning, when she was Darkness' male Light. And perhaps he still was her father, in all the ways that mattered. She saw Krane tapping her shoulder in another life, when she'd inhabited another body. *"Don't you take a break, boy!"* He'd said that so many times.

Krane lost his smile.

"No. No, the last time you saw me, in the shell I gave you, you told me I wasn't. You told me I was nothing to you. You were right to do so." The old male sighed. "I voted to kill the love of your life. I knew she was too dangerous. I just couldn't see past the fear. Took me a while to get past it. Took seeing my son die because of me."

Struggling to move, but needing to, she pulled away from Kai and wrapped her arms around her father, old, buried love coming through in waves.

"A thousand years. A thousand years, you plotted to get me back safe. Exiling yourself. The Nova, those who gave birth to me, gave me away. They had no choice, of course, but when I was five, they had another daughter. A replacement without magic. Then, they stopped visiting at all, pretending I was dead. I truly believed I had no family. But my *father* was there all along. With my mate, then with me."

He awkwardly wrapped his arms around her, and the rest of the world disappeared. Everything, except her father and Kai.

For a second, anyway.

Her heart well on its way to healing, she pulled at both of the males' sleeves. "Come on. We need to destroy that piece of junk."

"There's hundreds of fighters doing just that," Krane reminded her.

She turned to Kai. "Call them back."

Not questioning it, he gave the order through his comm. Through the translucent energy door leading out, she saw their ships returning to them.

"Get out of the hangar, and open the door from the command platform once you're safely in the contained zone," she instructed Krane.

Her father felt compelled to point out, "This is a

doorway leading to *space*. You will get pulled out and die in the cold, dark elements, in endless agony."

She rolled her eyes.

"Dramatic much? Open the damn door."

Krane gave up, muttering as he did what he was told.

She pushed to her tiptoes, kissing Kai, as the energy door opened. They needed no words; not after all this. They were one single mind. Their feet remained planted on the floor, their power anchoring them, and protecting them.

"I love you more than life itself. You're destruction. Darkness. Do what you do best."

She put her hands on either side of his head and surrendered all of her power to him.

Kai lifted his hand and smirked as golden strands of energy manifested, dancing out of his sleeve. They were quite beautiful, really. They gathered in one small ball in his palm. He pushed it out at full speed, straining a little as it transcended space, dividing to avoid their ships, then reforming and growing exponentially.

It hit the large, round, luminous Imperial StarX at full speed, and the skies were alight as thousands of souls perished, blown to pieces, just like she'd seen they would, long ago.

How stupid of her, thinking it had been an actual star.

Her hand was in Kai's, and she smiled, glad those beasts were gone.

She was Light, not a freaking saint.

"How about Evi?"

"We're not naming our daughter after you. You're already named her guardian if anything happens to us."

Nothing was going to happen to them. They were the two most powerful creatures in the universe, and they took care of each other, and, if that failed, Krane *had* managed to steal a full supply of rejuvenation serum before he'd left the Imperials high and dry. One shot went to Kai. The others were mostly given to Elia, head of tech development.

In her lab, the scientist worked on synthesizing it. Took a few years to manage, but now, those who earned it got a shot. Clera also got a few drops, so she could create a similar serum for animals.

Reluctantly, Nalini gave a shot to the neko when he was of age. She also finally named him. He was called Evil. It fit.

Satisfied with nothing short of excellence, Elia was still working on the serum, trying to find a way to make their immortality inherent, hereditary. She'd manage to change their genetic makeup within two hundred years, changing the face of the entire galaxy.

Kai was always worried, with good reason, knowing the Imperials had their eyes on them. They feared them, but fear was a weakness that, left unchecked, could cause a fair bit of devastation.

The inhabitants of their sector were the first to truly make themselves immortal.

He only grew more worried with time.

THEIR RACE DIDN'T LIKE to be associated with the Imperials. They were different in many ways. There was magic in their blood. Within a few generations, practically each one of their families had at least one mage. Their very nature made them wilder, needing that exchange of power to feed their magic. But they were also smarter. Faster. One of them was worth ten Imperials.

"Enlightened," Kronos proposed one day, when he'd

returned from his training on Tejen, a grown male with a lot of tricks up his sleeve.

He was lethal. His favorite weapon was manipulating time, because no one else managed to do so.

"We could be called Enlightened."

"That's pretty bigheaded," Nalini had to say.

Kai shrugged. "Maybe, but it fits."

And so, they were renamed.

THE YEAR NALINI gave birth to their twins, they made the decision that created a brand-new world.

Kai held Gaia in his arms, her little fingers wrapped around his thumb, as Nalini nursed Uranos. Daddy's girl and Mommy's boy. Twins.

Gaia wasn't just Kai's little treasure, though. She also was Kronos's. He picked her up as soon as someone put her down on her bed, ensuring that she'd be the most spoiled little thing in the world.

In a few hundred years, he'd marry her.

"WE NEED TO PROTECT THEM. The children. Our children's children. Those that come after. One day, the Empire will attack."

"And we will win," Nalini replied, but that didn't appease Kai.

They'd *probably* win. Probably wasn't enough now that he was a father.

"This galaxy is vast. There's a whole lot of unknown territory, and we both know the Imperials have stopped searching since they encountered the Ends-Day." A territory from which no one came back, marking the start of the unknown universe.

"You want to explore the unknown?"

One nod. Stiff.

"It's too dangerous."

She was no coward, but sending their subjects to their doom didn't appeal to her. "Volunteers only." He shrugged. "Some might dare it."

Nalini looked down at little Uranos.

"Volunteers only," she repeated, not expecting that once they were of age, both of her firstborns would wish to go.

The End

Next in Strands of Starfire: Hart's story, Diplomacy.

If you enjoyed this book, please leave a review. Book two will be scheduled if the ratings and number of reviews show enough interest.

Stay tuned for an excerpt of the Illustrated Companion to Strands of Starfire.

ACKNOWLEDGMENTS

I don't usually write these. No author is an island, I have an incredible team working with me, but, honestly, normally I just name them in my "credits" and that's it.

However, this is my longest, most complex, and, arguably, best book to date. It came about thanks to various people I truly wish to thank.

Firstly, thank you, **JC Andrijeski,** for listening to all my gushing about Joseph Campbell's Hero's Journey and watching video theories with me. You made this a blast.

Secondly, thank you, **Daniel Arenson.** After creating the word Starfire, I was scratching my head (and occasionally banging it against a wall) trying to find just the right title. And you handed it to me on a silver platter sprinkled with unicorn dust, so, you're the best.

Finally, I truly wish to thank every single member from **my Pack** for your encouragement, your critiques, and your patience. You ALWAYS (I know, I know. Me doing caps in a book! I must mean it) help me. Always. But Starfire was a journey I couldn't have taken without you.

Edited by Hot Tree Editing

Proofread by Susan Currin and Lisa Bing

Illustration by Jeremy Chong

Typography by Rebecca Frank

STRANDS OF STARFIRE: LINEAGE

UNEDITED EXCERPT

She came down the space ship alone. She'd never needed an escort of bodyguards; today was no exception, although she entered enemy territory.

Her mate, her advisors, and her friends had offered to come.

Not today.

There was nothing to fear. Nalini Krane Lor told herself that over and over as she walked the paved avenue separating the landing platform from the royal palace of Itri, home to the Nova, lords of the Var.

They'd assembled a welcoming committee. Hundreds of civilians, bowing to her as she passed them by, her head high, not sparing them a glance.

She couldn't look at them. Wouldn't.

They were treating her like she truly was the princess of this stinking hole, and for that reason, she wanted to yell, kick, and protest.

Some wounds never healed.

The palace's doors opened before she'd reached them. A still-beautiful, elegant female with raven hair burst out and held her hand up to her open mouth.

"Nalini," her mother whispered.

"Moa."

Her tone was entirely void of intonation. Of that, she was proud.

"I didn't think you'd truly come yourself."

There was so much feeling in her trembling voice. So much regret.

Nalini smiled. "Therein lays the difference between you and I, Moa. I don't turn my back on my blood. Where is my sister?"

ILLUSTRATED GLOSSARY - EXCERPT

The Black Lotus

Kai's ship, a customized Battria-X7 created by the Imperials, is a luxury light transport. Only two other models were sold in the Galaxy: the Emperor's, and Xera Krane's.

SKY

At two years of age, Sky killed her father, the previous Alpha of her pack, who took pleasure at eating pack-flesh.

When she met Kai in the winter, he was nothing more than an easy meal, until he communicated with her. Then, he became a strange, furless member of the pack.

His dominance level makes him a perfect Alpha, and that's just fine with her. She would never have taken the power if she hadn't needed to protect her wolves.

The Whistle

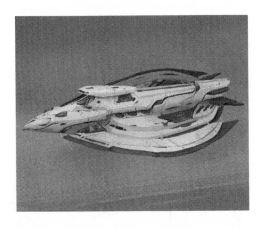

Nalini's ship, a Cn-1771 built in 1002 bought used, used to be part of a transport fleet dismantled sixty years later. They were deemed too slow and large. Less than a thousand of them were made, and only seven are currently operational.

The Whistle was extensively modified to make her faster than her peers.

More in the 150+ page illustrated glossary available on glossy hardback this spring! It includes illustrations of each term, character sketches, anecdotes and more.

AUTHOR'S NOTE

I truly hope that you loved Starfire, not only because I am absolutely in love with every aspect of this world, but because it explains a lot.

Strands of Starfire is an origin story to every single one of my series. In a few centuries, Kai and Nalini's children, along with other familiar names, will be leaving for Earth and my other worlds. I'll also write their journey at a later date.